Elizabeth Berg is the author of two highly praised works of fiction, *Durable Goods* and *Talk Before Sleep*. She lives in Massachusetts with her husband and two daughters

Critical acclaim for *Range of Motion*:

'Elizabeth Berg has written a beautiful book, steeped in grace, wit and compassion. *Range of Motion* tells a story so compelling that you wish it would never end, that you would never have to leave its vibrant, wise characters. When I came to the last page I simply turned back and started again. If you read one book this year, let it be this one. If you read one book next year, reread it'
Barbara Lazear Ascher, author of *The Habit of Loving*

'A love story that tells the truth about women and men'
Mary Kay Blakely, author of *American Mom*

'The voices of women with no-holds-barred honesty. The will-he-or-won't-he question drives the reader to turn pages almost too fast to catch the emotional resonance of this finely crafted work . . . so palpably full of loneliness and faith'
Publishers Weekly

'Berg's impeccable prose gives voice to that element in our psyche that enables us to cope with the impossible . . . Berg writes on a higher plane. We can't control life, Berg tells us, but it sure helps to have faith'
Booklist

'Readers who thought *The Bridges of Madison County* was a romantic book should try this story of honest and enduring love from the author of *Talk Before Sleep* . . . A touching and enjoyable read, this novel is romantic without being a romance'
Library Journal

Also by Elizabeth Berg

TALK BEFORE SLEEP
DURABLE GOODS

Range of Motion

Elizabeth Berg

BLACK SWAN

RANGE OF MOTION
A BLACK SWAN BOOK : 0 552 99716 1

First publication in Great Britain

PRINTING HISTORY
Black Swan edition published 1996

Grateful acknowledgement is made to the following for
permission to reprint previously published material:
Publishers Weekly: Excerpt from 'PW Interview: Barry Lopez'
(September 26, 1994). Reprinted by permission.
The University of Massachusetts Press: 'Summons' from *Robert
Francis: Collected Poems, 1936–1976* (Amherst: University of
Massachusetts Press, 1976). Copyright © 1976 by Robert Francis.
Reprinted by permission.

Set in 11pt Linotype Melior by
County Typesetters, Margate, Kent.

Black Swan Books are published by Transworld Publishers Ltd,
61–63 Uxbridge Road, London W5 5SA,
in Australia by Transworld Publishers (Australia) Pty Ltd,
15–25 Helles Avenue, Moorebank, NSW 2170,
and in New Zealand by Transworld Publishers (NZ) Ltd,
3 William Pickering Drive, Albany, Auckland.

Reproduced, printed and bound in Great Britain by
Cox & Wyman Ltd, Reading, Berks.

For you, holding this.

From me, nearby.

Keep me from going to sleep too soon
Or if I go to sleep too soon
Come wake me up. Come any hour
Of night. Come whistling up the road.
Stomp on the porch. Bang on the door.
Make me get out of bed and come
And let you in and light a light.
Tell me the northern lights are on
And make me look. Or tell me clouds
Are doing something to the moon
They never did before, and show me.
See that I see. Talk to me till
I'm half as wide awake as you
And start to dress wondering why
I ever went to bed at all.
Tell me the walking is superb.
Not only tell me but persuade me.
You know I'm not too hard persuaded.

—ROBERT FRANCIS, 'SUMMONS'

I think that the world desires to be beautiful. I have found that beauty in mathematics. I have found it in the hunting behavior of wolves, and the way men and women touch each other. I think the world's keenest desire is for beauty, and that our knowledge of how to achieve that is the various forms of behaviour and expression that we apply a single word to, which is love.

—BARRY LOPEZ

Acknowledgments

My thanks, as always, to my agent, Lisa Bankoff, and to my editor, Kate Medina, who take such good care of me.

My Tuesday morning writers' group does everything a writers' group should, and more. I love them and I appreciate them and I owe them more than I can ever repay.

Jessica Treadway and Bill Kahn were early readers who took time away from busy schedules to give to me, and I appreciate it.

Range of Motion

Prologue

They say that one of the reasons for tragedy is that you learn important lessons from it. Appreciation for your normal life, for one thing. A new longing for things only ordinary. The feeling is that we are so caught up in minutiae – slicing tomatoes and filling out forms and waiting in lines and emptying the dryer and looking in the paper for things to do – that we forget how to use what we've been given. Therefore we don't taste the plum. We are blind to the slant of the four o'clock sun against the changing show of leaves. We are deaf to the throaty purity of children's voices. We are assumed to be rather hopeless – swallowed up by incorrect notions, divorced from the original genius with which we are born, lost within days of living this distracting life. We are capable only of moments, of single seconds of true appreciation and connection. That is the thought.

I never did believe that. I always felt I had a

kind of continual appreciation with a flame that did not flicker, despite the ongoing assaults of an imperfect life. I didn't think I was the only one, either. I thought that all around me were awake people with hearts huge and whole and open. And I wondered, after the accident happened, what is the point in this? Where is the meaning in it? What lesson can I possibly learn?

But sometimes lessons take the crooked path. I mean that I used to wonder how I would feel if I were suddenly plucked from my normal life. I wondered how I would see it; wondered, in fact, *if* I would see it. I suppose it's like the desire for a true mirror to reflect all of our parts, both visible and unseen. I think now the accident was a way of that happening. Because I did get plucked from my normal life, put in the position of seeing it from another vantage point. And I would say that I did see it. I would say that I saw and saw and saw it. And though the method is not one I would have chosen to verify a supposition, I would also say that my gratefulness is unutterable.

I can tell you how it happened. It's easy to say how it happened. He walked past a building, and a huge chunk of ice fell off the roof, and it hit him in the head. This is Chaplinesque, right? This is kind of funny. People start to laugh when I tell them. I see the start of their hand to their mouth, their poor disguise. I laughed when I heard. I thought after the doctor told me what happened that Jay would get on the phone and say, 'Jeez, Lainey, come and get me. I've got a goose egg the size of the world. Come take me home.' Only what happened wasn't like Chaplin: Jay didn't land on his butt with his legs sticking out at chopstick angles, twitch his mustache, get back up and walk away. He landed on his side, and stayed there — rather like a child sleeping, the ambulance attendant told the doctor. He was on his side, his arm draped peacefully across his chest, and he didn't wake up at the hopsital nor has he since.

Now there is no ice on buildings. Now daffodils sway, uncertain in their newness. Now the hospital is going to transfer him to a nursing home. No more they can do, they told me in our little meeting this morning. 'Wait,' I said. 'There has to be more.' I wanted a bigger conference, one of those fancy ones where the social worker comes and tries not to let me see her looking at her watch. It's a tacky watch. You shouldn't try to make a watch look like a bracelet. One or the other. But anyway, Wait, I said, and they said, Sorry, Mrs Berman, we just can't keep him. I said nothing after that. I thought I would sit there saying nothing until they gave in and said okay. They didn't do that. They left, one by one. I saw the white coat of the neurologist flapping a bit as he walked past, the head nurse looking at notes she pulled out of her pocket. I heard the squeak of the physical therapist's new sneakers, Nikes, he'd said yesterday, he always buys Nikes, and we'd talked about the relative merits of sneakers and I'd watched the sun play off the top of his hair while he gave Jay range of motion. That is what they call the passive exercise Jay gets here, range of motion. He can no longer jog every morning, returning on Sundays with a bag from Lessinger's bakery that smells of warm sugar and is stained with irresistible patterns of translucence from the grease. He can't move at all. So every day, a few times a day, someone must put each of Jay's body parts through all the movements of which they are capable. First the thumb is bent, then straightened, then bent and straightened again, twice more. Next, each finger is done individually; then the whole hand, fingers all together. Then comes the wrist, then the elbow, and so on. They do his neck, they do his knees, they do his great toes and his little ones. *Don't forget*, a stranger's hand tells Jay's body. *Remember all that is here for you to use.* So I was watching and I was telling the therapist I still liked Keds, but I was thinking, Be careful. And I was thinking, Save him.

Saving was not on the agenda at the meeting. They were not really thinking of Jay. What they were thinking was, Next? This left me no time to tell them that they were dismissing the man who showed up at my dorm room with his arms full of lilacs, stolen at considerable risk and so purple the buds were black. He wore a white shirt with the sleeves rolled up to the good place, and a heart-shaped leaf lay trapped in the hollow of his throat as though it were planned, though of course it was so perfect it couldn't have been planned. He was nineteen then. Now he is thirty-five, the father of two children who hang on his arms when he comes home, fight for the privilege of relieving him of his briefcase. Girls, Amy and Sarah, four and ten, who are beginning to yell at me because they miss their father.

I go to visit him every day and I keep trying. Jay, I say. You need to come back here now. Please come back. Wake up. I put things in his hands for him to feel: his wallet and keys, his cotton work shirt worn to the softness of Kleenex, baby pinecones, his daughters' drawings, the comb from my hair, a fork. I talk almost nonstop, about anything, just so that the language might stir him, just so that something, a word, an image, might reach the deep and silent place in him that surely is waiting for the right thing, which will be tiny, I know, which will be so tiny and amaze everyone. 'How did you do it?' they'll say and I'll say, 'Listen. There isn't a way. It was a normal day. I turned an afternoon movie on his television. Black and white. Bette Davis. I started to tell him to pay attention, this was a good part, and he woke up. That's all. That's it. You just have to wait. You just have to believe.'

I would guess that they have given up on believing, here. They have seen too many coma patients die – 'fail,' they call it – even when all signs pointed toward recovery.

Now I will wait in a nursing home and I will probably be the only one who believes. It will be around my head like a pale aura, my belief, but at the nursing home they will no doubt see my hope only as naïveté and it will make them more tired than they already are. 'Pardon me,' I see them saying, their arms full of scorched linens, giving me wide berth and not looking me in the eye lest I ask another question. I've heard about nursing homes. Imagine how many flowers I'll have to bring to cover up the stench of urine.

When Jay brought me those lilacs, there was a

20

cut all along the underside of his forearm, a line of valor like a red road on a map. I had to wrap my arms around myself at the sight of it. I thought it was the most romantic thing I'd ever seen. But that was nothing.

I've thought: his name should have been a little longer. Lionel. Joshua. Richard. Then when he signed the checks for the bills he was going to mail on the way to work that morning, it would have taken a little longer. And the ice would have fallen before he got there. He would have walked around it, admired the cool blue color trapped in the white. I've thought: we should have made love that morning. He should have gone to the hardware store before work. The dentist. He should have gone in earlier than usual. Often I've thought: this is for something I did.

This is what you do. Also, sometimes, you sleep.

After the conference about Jay going to the nursing home, I sat on the bed beside him and pushed his hair back from his forehead. 'Hey, guess what?' I said. 'You're moving!' I felt like a very cheerful person saying to another, 'Well! Your house has exploded! Isn't *that* nice!'

I feel you sitting down beside me. I smell your hair. Is it . . . are we at the breakfast table, your blue robe? I nearly start the reach but then there is the other. A high whine of wind. Speed, this hurtling forward. Red weeds standing straight below me, an evenness of the space between them. I see the black earth, mica, the start of

21

stars. I am tunneling deeper toward all that calls.
Things move aside, let me in. Lainey, my bones
have gone soft and flat, spread out into useless-
ness. I have to pay attention. I can't tell you. But I
feel you. Stay.

I live in a duplex outside of St Paul. It's a big old house, on a city street lined by trees that survived the last round of Dutch elm disease. I had to have the place as soon as I saw it. I felt at home there, even with the rooms empty and echoing. I felt enveloped, at the end of some journey. I turned to Jay and said, 'Yes, here.' And he said, 'I thought so.'

Someone once told me she saw a house from the highway that she recognized, though she had never seen it before. She said she felt sure that if she went in, she'd know her way around, that she'd be able to predict where the line of sun and shadow met in every room. She didn't stop, though. She turned on the radio, changed lanes, sped up. As we do.

There's a lot of wood inside my house, golden oak. There are big bedrooms with creaky floors and high ceilings; a pantry in the kitchen, double windows over the sink. There are decals that someone put on the kitchen cabinets, featuring cream-colored mixing bowls with blue stripes and dancing wooden spoons. I like those decals. I have an ongoing romance with the time that they were popular. I like everything about the forties: the music, the flowered tablecloths, the snub-nosed cars, the skirts on the voluptuous armchairs, the purses with the handles that you carried when you wore gloves and open-toed heels and a hat with a veil. I always tell everybody that's my real time, the forties, the time I was meant to live in. Jay says I did. He says he lived then, too, and we were sweethearts, and he was killed in the Solomon Islands during World War II. He was kidding. Kind of. We play a lot of big-band music: Glenn Miller. Tommy Dorsey. Les Brown, Harry James. We play records of Peggy Lee before she sounded like Peggy Lee.

There was an old wringer-washer in the basement when we moved in, and I left it there. I like to imagine a ghost woman standing beside it, wearing a loose-fitting housedress and an apron, the pockets holding a floral handkerchief and bobby pins and the tiny fortune of coins pulled from behind the sofa cushions each day. I like to think about her catching a severely flattened shirt as it came from the wringer, then putting it in a wicker basket and carrying it outside to hang on the rope clothesline. When it got dry and scented by air and sunshine, she would iron it, sprinkling it first by dipping her fingers in a pan, then

24

shaking the drops around like holy water. After she slid the warm shirt onto the hanger, she would hold it at arm's length, inspect it with the fond strictness of a mother.

I like to imagine this woman's whole life in this house: the line of hair escaping to blow across her face as she stood on the steps calling the kids in to dinner, the smell of her roast in the oven, potatoes browning and carrots curling in the blue-and-white-speckled Dutch oven. She wore long white nightgowns to bed; I won't have it any other way. She wrote out her grocery list with a stubby yellow pencil her husband brought home from the insurance company where he worked. Ovaltine, she wrote, in school-correct script. Butter. 'Chattanooga Choo-Choo' came from the yellowish-white radio on top of the refrigerator. At ten-thirty in the morning, her phone would ring, the black and clunky phone sitting on the hall table on a doily, a fat phone book on the helpful shelf below. 'Hello?' she would say, and then she'd listen to an invitation to have coffee with a neighbor. 'That'd be swell,' she'd say, and she'd take off her cleaning kerchief and walk across the street. She would sit at her neighbor's kitchen table with her legs crossed, talking, talking, hearing the pleasant china sound of her cup nesting into the saucer.

The women were home. They got to talk. I'm not sure it wasn't better. Think of it, the luxury of talking to another woman and feeling your three-year-old idly pressing his head into your stomach, instead of being fined for picking him up late at day care – again.

I don't know. I keep these things mostly to myself. I keep the ghost woman for myself. Oh, I've told Jay how I think it might have been better before. I've told him that. I've said sometimes I long so hard for older times. He always understands. He likes applesauce with pork chops. He likes this house for its old-fashionedness as much as I; he didn't mind keeping the wringer-washer.

I've told Jay just about everything, from the day I met him. He is the way I determine where to put everything on the scale: Is this crazy? Is this right? Isn't this funny?

When we were younger, in our twenties, we lived together before we got married. Before we went to sleep at night, we used to hold hands and sing little made-up songs to each other about what we did that day. 'First I got up, and I looked out the window, and I saw a little bird . . .' I would sing. And then he sang about what he did. His melody was not as good as mine – he's no singer, Jay – but he would sing about what he saw on the way to work and what he did there and what he ate for lunch and what happened on the way home and it was all very silly but it was surprising, too, what the songs told us. I suppose they were a kind of shy testimony to the love we had for each other and for the life we were living. 'Telling Songs,' we called them.

We did it for a long time, until I ruined it. We had vowed never to tell anyone about it, imagine the embarrassment. Then one night I secretly tape-recorded Jay singing to me. I played it back to him and we both laughed. But then he made me tape over it, right away. His song got covered up with the sounds of us breathing, talking a little, an ambulance siren got on there – and after that we just stopped singing to each other. I don't know if I really ruined it by taping him. I think I might have sensed that our singing was coming to an end soon, and I wanted to preserve some little bit of it. But I couldn't tape him without telling him I'd done it and then he was just too embarrassed to let me keep it around. I wish now, of course, that I had at least kept that recording of us doing nothing, of us trying to conceal our tender secrets. I do sleep with a shirt of his that I had the good sense not to launder. Sometimes you know before you know.

I have a good neighbor, in every sense of the word. Alice, her name is. She lives with her husband, Ed. He's a distant man, cool in a way that is perhaps unintentional. It's not that he doesn't smile; it's that if his smile were something you drew, you'd erase it, thinking, Wrong. They have a seven-year-old son named Timothy, never called Timmy or Tim; a little, scrawny guy who wears thick glasses already, and who tucks his striped T-shirts into his pants with the aplomb of a silver-templed CEO. I like him very much. I think he's going to be a great Something in science. He knows the word *cache*, he could read at three. I think he's a genius, actually. 'Nah,' Alice says, meaning, 'I couldn't agree with you more.'

Alice is the most unattractive woman I have ever seen. She has a complexion that went on a rampage in her teens and never settled down. Her hair is forever frizzed; nobody can do anything about it and everyone has tried. She has too-big lips, which I know are all the rage now, but not on Alice; and she has muddy brown eyes that are too small. She's not overweight, but there are no cheekbones in sight on her face, no bones at all. One thing that's nice are her ears, which are shell-like, really very pleasant to look at. But of course that's not enough.

Still, there is something about her. She's the hardest person to explain. If you saw her, the first thing you'd do is think, my God, she's so ugly, and you'd feel sort of guilty, feel sorry for her. But then you'd look again. And all that feeling sorry for her would be gone, because of what is in her that is so strong, and clear, and finished. You would want to talk to her. You would want her to know you, and to approve of you. You would believe that in her hands, things were safe. And brushing at the back of your shamed brain would be some new knowledge about our usual concept of beauty, namely, the extreme wrongness of it.

Alice is sitting out on the wide front steps of our duplex now, smoking, and she watches me get out of the car and come toward her. I see that the sun is low in the sky; it must be nearly six o'clock. I'm late. I step over the weeds that are just beginning to poke out of the cracks of the sidewalk. They're kind of pretty at first, and welcome, the way all green things are in early spring. In a few weeks, we'll be paying the kids a penny apiece to pull them out. Well, we'll pay Timothy and Amy. Sarah won't do it anymore unless we pay her a dollar apiece. Which we won't do. It occurs to me that there was ice on the sidewalk the last time I heard Jay's voice, and the thought is like the pinch of skin in zipper.

Alice doesn't smoke inside my house and only rarely in her own. She smokes on the porch, even in the winter. I'll see her sitting out there in the morning, a parka over her nightgown, galoshes over her wild-colored knee socks. She drinks her coffee quickly so it doesn't freeze, then smokes her cigarette even faster, so she doesn't. Before coming in, she does five quick jumping jacks. This is so she can tell her doctor that yes indeed, she exercises daily. She counts her numbers out loud, as though you could lose track counting up to five. Her tone is serious. She is her own drill sergeant.

She watches me carefully; then, when I am closer, smiles and juts her chin out at me, a greeting. She puts her cigarette out in the clay ashtray Timothy made. It's orange and lumpy, the kind of thing any parent loves.

I sit down beside her, offer her a bouquet of tulips. They are a beautiful silky red color, with show-off streaks of yellow running up the center of each petal. She grabs them out of my hand, then frowns at me. 'Why do you do this?' she says. 'You're starting to piss me off.' And then, 'Thank you.'

Well, she does so much, I want to bring her little presents now and then. She's been taking care of my kids every day since January 17th; now it's

April 21st. She says she doesn't mind, she says what the hell's the difference, she lives right here, the kids go to the same school, she's not doing anything. But of course she is. Even when you like other people's kids, they're still other people's kids. You have to be a little more alert, a little nicer, it makes for a strain. I'd like to give her more than tulips. She deserves a piece of the glowing moon, captured in a jar.

'Don't be pissed off,' I tell her now. 'Just put them by your bed. When you wake up and see them, you'll feel happy.' From out back, I hear the chatter of the kids. I lean forward, turn my head so that I can hear them better.

'They're building a spaceship,' Alice says. 'They have to finish before bedtime, so you can imagine how busy they are. I wonder how they'll protect the cardboard when they get close to the sun. Incidentally, we had tuna noodle casserole for dinner, don't sue me.'

'I like tuna noodle casserole. So do they. Thank you. I didn't know what the hell to feed them tonight. Last night we had spaghetti with butter, and cucumber slices.'

'Your kids are fine,' Alice says, though of course she knows they are not, not really, not mine. Mine are having a few little problems. Amy has begun wetting her bed; Sarah is hostile to me, and she seems to have forgotten every bit of math she ever learned, including addition. 'I wouldn't worry about it just now,' her teacher told me, her lipstick precisely within the lines of her mouth, her blouse ironed. I looked at her normality as if it were a museum exhibit.

'So how's Jay?' Alice asks. I notice she is wearing mascara, a first. I want to talk about that. I want to say, Why, Alice! You're wearing make-up! Do you like it? Yes, I want to talk about makeup, tell Alice how the cheap mascara is always the best and I hope she didn't go to some department-store dowager and pay twenty dollars for it. I want to talk about what movies are playing, what kind of marinade is best for salmon, what was on the front page of the newspaper. Instead, I look down at my feet and say, 'They're going to move him to a nursing home tomorrow.'

'What? *Why?*'

'Well, you know. They said they can't keep him past a certain number of days when he's making no progress.' I look at her. 'He's making no progress. He's flunking out.'

'Well. He's still alive. They don't know every-thing. He could come back at any moment. People do.'

'Yeah, I know.' I pull the tie off my ponytail, shake out my hair. It's dirty. I wonder when I washed it last.

'So where are they taking him?'

'Ridgeview,' I say. 'Over on Grand Street. It's what I can afford. It's probably a pit. Oh, God, this is awful. I hate this. He's got to hurry up and get better, now. I can't keep this up forever.'

Alice wraps her arms around herself, rocks back and forth slightly. How we speak when we don't speak. I watch her moving shoulder, note with a kind of pleasure the small rip in the sleeve of her purple cardigan.

'They changed his feeding tube today,' I say, in a voice that I might use to mention a sale on London broil at Buy Rite.

'Oh yeah? That's good.'

'Jesus, Alice,' I say then, and the lightness I attempted with my voice feels snatched from me, as though I'd been caught stealing it. 'I just . . .' I say. And then, 'Well, you know, I . . .' And then I stop talking, put my hands over my face. They smell like dirt and metal.

She reaches over to put her arm around me. 'Right,' she says softly. 'I know.' I start to cry and then I stop; and then I get up to go around back to see what the kids are doing.

On my side, they're rolling me onto my side. A ship, lolling in the waves. Green fronds, the mouths of fish, the pull of the moon. I see you in your yellow dress, Lainey, the rip at the shoulder and how your tanned summer fingers felt along the line of it, as if to repair by touch. Dizzy. The spinning beginning. Low sound, thunder? I see the red blood cells passing, platelike disks, the opening and closing of the minute blossoms in my lungs. I am trying, but I am wrapped in so many layers. Here, a flash and a click. Light. An electric buzz. 'So what's going on after work?' I hear. I hear! What effort it is to breathe. Am I breathing?

*　　　*　　　*

'It's to save us from the end of the world, when it blows up,' Sarah says, looking at me and shielding her eyes from the last bit of the lowering sun. She has laid a long branch carefully on top of another. She turns back, busy with the tasks at hand, bored with me already, me standing there with no good news, it's plain to see.

She's a very pretty little girl, Sarah, with her black eyebrows and light hair and perfect face. Her last birthday brought a new air of confidence that makes me a little uncomfortable with her lately. I see her as beginning to develop into the kind of girl whose yearbook picture every parent points to, saying, 'And who's *that*?' Jay and I agreed that we didn't exactly know where Sarah came from, though he watched this change with a kind of prideful delight rather than with my wariness.

Amy comes to lean against my leg and watch the others work. Here's the little girl I can still relate to, the one with the stick-out ears and cowlicks and love of garlic bread and dandelions. She puts her thumb in her mouth, reaches skillfully with the same hand for a bit of her hair. I lift her up, smell the sweet wrinkle in her neck, stop myself from saying, 'Help me, I'm so tired.'

'Where's Daddy?' she says. She always asks, as if it's a surprise that he hasn't stepped out of the car along with me.

'He's still in the hospital, honey. But tomorrow he gets to move to a new place.'

She pulls away to look at my face. 'Where?'

'It's a place called Ridgeview. It's a nursing

home. And maybe he'll wake up there, and then we can bring him home.'

'Why?'

'Why would we bring him home? Because he'll be better then.'

'No. Why will he wake up there?'

'Well, I don't know if he will. But maybe he will because it's just a different place. Maybe it will stimulate him.'

She lays her head back down, thinks about this. As do I. Maybe he will wake up there! Maybe so! Sometimes I think this is why we have kids, to create hope for ourselves.

'Mom!' Sarah calls. 'Can I use some Saran Wrap?'

'Sure,' I say. How easy some things are. What a relief it is to come home, to be able to do something about something.

'Sarah?'

She looks up. 'What?'

'Never mind,' I say. 'I'll bring it out to you.' I just wanted to see her respond when I called her name, is the truth. 'Can I help build?' I ask.

'Yeah, you can do the floor,' Timothy says. 'It has to be really sturdy.' He pushes his glasses up onto the bridge of his nose, scratches absent-mindedly at his wrist. I can see him thirty years from now, white-coated, staring into a micro-scope, too intent on his genius to eat his paper-bag lunch. Inside Alice's kitchen, I hear her and Ed talking, the sound floats out over us. I feel a stab of jealousy.

'No, you can't help!' Sarah tells me. And then, to Timothy, 'She can't.'

'Why not?' he asks.

'Because she *can't*.' She stares fiercely at him.

He shrugs in the huge way of children. 'Well, *I* don't care.'

'It's okay,' I say. 'I need to make some phone calls anyway. I'll bring you the Saran Wrap, but then finish up for today. You can only stay out for another few minutes.'

I hike Amy up higher on my hip, go into the kitchen and notice the smell of my own house, which I'd forgotten. Something like toast. And Pledge, I actually cleaned a little yesterday. I know why Sarah doesn't want me to help. She thinks I'll mess up. This is my reputation lately. Courtesy of an accident that happened to someone else.

I get the Saran Wrap, ask Amy to take it outside. I want to change clothes. 'When you come back in, you can have a bubble bath,' I tell her.

'And two stories, you said last night I could have two.'

'And that's exactly what you'll get,' I said. 'I promised, I know. I'll do what I promised, don't worry about it.'

Alice and Ed have a little dog named Maggie. She looks like an animal dressed up like a dog, like a hedgehog or a weasel wearing a Tina Turner wig. I keep a bowl out for her; she visits. Lately, I've been holding her in my lap in the rocker, moving back and forth, feeling the little shakes her panting makes. I pet her whole body with long, slow strokes. She's awful, really, her pop-out eyes, her rough fur, her awesomely bad breath. I can't imagine what kind of dogs produced her. I can't imagine why I love to rock her so. Last night, I put her over my shoulder like a newborn – she's about the same size – and watched the half-moon out the window while we creaked back and forth in the rhythm that all women know from secrets whispered to their genes at the time of their conception. I was thinking, I am a female person with freckles scattered across the back of my hands, living under a sky that changes at random.

I can only look up. Everything stops there, with my trusting that the asking is going somewhere. I felt a rush of longing flood through me as though water were rising on my insides to the top of my brain. And then Maggie all of a sudden jumped over my shoulder like Superdog and ran to the back door, shaking herself as though she'd just been bathed. As though she was trying to get rid of some sorrow she'd caught from me.

I don't see Maggie around tonight. I've got nobody. The kids are asleep, half-washed. What are you doing, Jay? Where are you?

What are you doing, Lainey? Where are you?

Jay rode to the nursing home in an ambulance. Two hospital orderlies loaded him onto the gurney, a nice, shiny one, capable of tricks like rising up and down at the flick of a finger. They covered him with hospital blankets, then pushed him down the hall, his few personal things in a plastic bag that, at first, they had resting on his chest as though he were a hall table. 'Please,' I said, and moved the bag to his side, as it would be if he were really carrying it.

The orderlies looked at each other. One of them had gum, and he'd stopped chewing it out of respect for me. But then, because I'd embarrassed him, he started chewing again. He blew a bubble in my direction. I wanted to slap his ignorant face. Instead I said nothing until I saw the ambulance attendants coming up to take over, and then I asked them to wait, to let me follow them. I wanted to be right behind.

And so here we are, driving down the highway, past the ruined beauty of downtown. Even in Minnesota, this has happened. I'm scared to go into the city at night. Even when I was with Jay that was true. I like to take a cab, get dropped off right in front of where we're going. It's only recent, this fear. I used to take the kids to the city with me all the time, to look in the big department stores, to sit on bus-stop benches and watch the people. Jay's mother is from New York and she says things are so different there, and in such a short length of time. She said she used to get dressed up to ride the subway. We don't go to New York very often, but when we do and we ride the subway, I'm afraid. Jay said it was because I'm getting old. I say it's because the world has changed irrevocably. If the boom boxes were quiet at the subway stations, I would still hear that kind of music there.

We pull into the nursing-home driveway and I park in the visitor's lot, which is almost empty, which is exactly what I mean about nursing homes. I've driven past this place before, but now that Jay's going in it on a gurney, it looks entirely different.

The attendants wheel Jay to the nurse's desk. There's no one there. They ring a bell on the chest-high counter, and a harried young thing comes around the corner. She's wearing a nurse's hat, which I haven't seen in a long time. It looks sort of stupid, like she ought to be on a sitcom. Curls from her permed hair leak out around it. She yells

40

down the hall, 'Gloria! Your admission's here!' and then she comes up to discuss Jay's paperwork with the ambulance attendants. She tells me she'll be with me in a moment. When the attendants have finished, they walk past me, nodding grimly, both of them; and then they wait, leaning against the wall, for the return of the gurney. It's a funny thing, but I'm scared to give it back to them. Then Jay will not be connected to the hospital anymore.

It's twelve noon. Probably the ambulance attendants will go eat lunch after this. On their minds will be what to order. They see this kind of thing all the time, people in comas. They won't wonder about us, they won't tell their wives about us at dinner.

The nurse comes up to me, holds out her hand. 'I'm Pat Swanson,' she says. 'I'm the head nurse here. You're the wife?'

I nod. I'm the wife. 'Elaine,' I say. 'Berman.' God, I'm tired. I feel like my blood is mercury. I feel like my brain is a big steel square.

'Right. Nice to meet you. We'll be putting him into his room – it's number 203 – and then you can come in. It'll take just a minute.'

I repeat the number to myself. It occurs to me that perhaps I should write it down, so that I don't have to come in here next time and ask, 'Where did you say my husband is again?'

I stand there, watching, as they push him down the hall. His foot has come uncovered, and this hurts my feelings. His room is third on the right, close to the nurses' station. Well, that's good. I wait, staring out the windows so that I don't have to look at any of the patients here. I've heard Jay isn't the youngest, but I don't see any evidence of that. There are a few very old people out in the hall in wheelchairs, most of them with restraint jackets on. One woman holds her purse on her lap, a squarish black patent-leather thing, and I have the sad feeling that it is probably empty. Well, maybe a handkerchief. Yellow lozenges covered with lint. She stares straight ahead, calm, impassive. She looks like she's waiting for a bus. An old man sits near her, his head hanging, drooling onto his checkered shirt and weeping soundlessly. My God. I'll go crazy leaving Jay here. I can't leave him here. I can't bring him home. I can't leave him here.

I take in a breath, head toward Jay's room, meet Pat coming out. 'He's all set,' she says. 'You can go in. I need to call his doctor to clear up one of his orders, and then I'll be back in. You'll have to answer a few questions for me.'

He was walking past a building, I'll say. Just like you do every day. I'm so tired of telling the story. At first, it was interesting to me. I wanted not to forget any of the details, so I could tell them to Jay when he came home and was soaking in the bathtub with a washcloth on top of his head. He used to like to put a hot washcloth there, let the steam rise as though his brains were cooling. It was a fantastic novelty at first, having a husband in a coma because ice knocked him out. It was a challenge to overcome, and I thought we might even go on television when it was all over, describe the way faith and magic got us through. 'So, did you pray a lot, Mrs Berman?' Oprah would ask me and I'd say, Please call me Elaine and then I'd say, 'Well, not prayer, really. No, I didn't pray. But I believed.' I do. I do still believe.

I go to the side of Jay's bed, touch his hand, kiss his cheek. 'Here we are,' I say. 'This is the new place, where you'll get better, Jay.' I put my hands to his face, fingers meeting in the middle of his forehead, then run them lightly over his eyelids, down along his cheekbones, into the curl of his ears. I smooth his hair along his temples, then run my hands along the back of his head, lifting his neck slightly, then letting it fall back into the pillow. A little massage. My love, translated.

Out the back of my head, the release of galaxies. From my mouth, oceans and granite. From my nose, the curl of new ferns, walls of roses. Climbing out of my ears, zebras, antelope, two by two. Out of my hair, dandelions and grapevines, spiders with stiff silk legs, reaching forth and testing with every normal step. Under the lids of my eyes, the sky, the arching up of a million rainbows.

'I'm here,' I whisper, my mouth close to his ear, and I see the sound going deeper, going somewhere I can't, spreading out like ripples on water.

I straighten up, rub hard at the small of my back, look around. The room is private, small. The curtains at the window are a brown-and-yellow print and a big tear in the corner of one of

43

them has been sloppily repaired. Maybe these things make a difference. Maybe I'll make some curtains to hang here that have been rubbed across my skin, and the girls', and I'll hem them by hand, think healing thoughts with each stitch.

There's an orange plastic chair for the visitor parked in the corner. I pull it forward, station it by Jay's side. I'll bring a throw for it, a pillow.

I feel a slight breeze, notice that the window is cracked open. Outside, spring comes in spite of everything. There are moments when we think nature happens just for us, and there are other moments when the ridiculousness of that notion is revealed.

The sun is falling on Jay's face. I turn his head slightly, so the light won't be in his eyes. I see a spot near his left ear where they missed shaving him this morning. His beard just keeps growing. I touch the stiff hairs, remember so much in a moment I think I might choke.

Alice calls at eight o'clock that night. 'I know you're in your pajamas,' she says. 'Get out of them. You're going out with me. We're going to a bar.'

I am stunned, silent.

'I mean it,' she says. 'You have not been out one time since this happened.'

'Well. Because I don't want to.'

'But you need to. You *need* to. Here: *I* need to, okay? Does that make it better? I'm bored over here, it's boring. I want to go do something. Ed said he'd babysit, he'll bring Timothy over, he can fall asleep there. It's Friday night. Let's go tip a few. You just have to promise not to be jealous when all the guys hit on me.'

'I don't think so, Alice.'

'What are you going to do instead?'

Stare into the night. Think. Maybe weep, although you'd think something would have dried up by now. Try to figure out how much insurance coverage we've got left from Jay's computer company. Try to figure out if I have to go back to work yet. 'Okay,' I say. 'But just to O'Gara's. Just for a little while.' O'Gara's is the bar a few blocks from us. It's a neighborhood joint, lace curtains, brass rails, hamburgers served on thick tan plates. We took the kids there once, sat in a booth. Jay let the kids taste beer. Sarah screwed up her face; Amy asked for more. We said no, we told her she could watch *Peter Pan* that night instead. We all did. We all got in our pajamas and watched the ticking of the clock prey on Hook's nerves.

I go into Sarah's bedroom; she and Amy are playing Barbies there. Tiny killer heels and formal gowns turned inside out litter the floor. A naked Ken lies lonely on the periphery. They don't like him. His head pops off all the time.

'You should get into your pajamas,' I say.

'It's not a school night,' Sarah says, and Amy repeats it mindlessly after her, concentrating on the aggravating closures of the tight skirt she's trying to fit a doll into. I think it's the one they call Helen, whom they have made a librarian. Bless their hearts, I have done something right.

'I'm going out,' I say, and they both look up, then freeze, as though they have become photographs of themselves.

'With Alice. Just for a little while.'

'Where are you going?' Amy says.

'Just over to O'Gara's.'

'Oh.' She refocuses on her doll.

Sarah says nothing, looks coolly away from me.

'Do you mind?' I ask her. And echoing behind that is, Am I so different to you now? Do you hate me? What is it? Is it your father? Is it your age? Is it inevitable? '*Do* you mind?' I ask again. I nursed you. I had you. I love you. Where are you?

'I don't mind,' she says. And then, 'Is someone babysitting us?'

'Actually Ed's just going to come over, with Timothy.'

Sarah's eyes widen. 'I don't want a *man*!'

'It'll be fine. You can all play a game.'

'That's what you always say. You think it's so good to play games. Nobody even likes games. And I am *not* putting on my pajamas!'

'Fine. You can wait until I get home. At which time we will have a little chat about how we talk to our mothers.'

'I'm not putting on my pajamas either,' Amy says, and for a moment attempts a look of indignation she doesn't quite understand the reason for. Then she hands me the doll. 'Can you snap that? And make her a bun?'

I take the doll from her, get busy. I still like playing with dolls. The longer their hair is, and the blonder, the more excited I get. 'Is this what she's wearing?' I ask Amy when I've finished the hairdo. I see a lot of things I like better in the pile. The pink gown with the fabric rose at the waist, for instance.

'Mom,' Amy says. 'Give her back.'

I go into the bathroom, run a brush through my hair. Should I put on makeup? He can't even turn on a light. He can't even turn over.

Who is it? Who's calling me?

Bars never change. Neon light. Older patrons lined up over their drinks, shirtsleeves rolled up, cigarette smoke undulating at their sides. Younger patrons flirting, the women tossing hair back and raising chins to reveal their necks and their earrings. And their availability. Alice and I sit at the end of the bar and we haven't even gotten our drinks when someone is on the bar stool beside me. I can feel him looking at me and then he says, '*You* haven't been here before.'

You know, I am not spectacular-looking, but I do have long, blond hair and it gets them every time. Jayne Mansfield, they're thinking. Marilyn Monroe. And then you turn around and you're not like that, but they've gotten started so they just keep going.

I turn fully toward him: blue eyes, dimple in his chin, curly brown hair, faded blue work shirt open a couple of buttons. Maybe he's a carpenter. I once was friends with a carpenter who used to tell me about all the housewives he seduced when he was wild and single. They would have coffee with him and tell him everything. One woman had had a mastectomy and she told him all about it. He said he fell in love with her and once he kissed her and felt her up a little and she pulled away and smiled into his face and said, 'That's the wrong one.'

I start to say something to the man beside me, I start to say something like, No thank you, but the whole thing is just too ridiculous. I turn away without saying anything, roll my eyes at Alice.

'So what brings you here?' he asks the back of my head. The persistent type.

I look at him. 'My husband is in a coma. The grief is driving me crazy. I needed a break.'

The man pulls back a little, nods knowingly while he tongues off his back teeth. Then he says, 'That's not funny.'

'It certainly isn't.'

'You all have a nice night,' he says, and leaves. The bar stool he vacates revolves back and forth slightly, then stops.

Alice takes a long drink of her beer. 'I told you they'd be all over me,' she says. 'But what are you going to do?' She is wearing her cowboy shirt, something she found in the Salvation Army. It features a number of men wearing chaps and spurs and huge white hats, whirling lassos. Some of the cowboys face forward, grinning; some are seen from behind. Branding irons float in the background, and a brand, too, A&S. I asked Alice if she liked cowboys, when she first showed me that shirt. I was hoping she did, because I love cowboys. As a little girl, I'd written many love letters to Roy Rogers, which I never mailed out of respect for Dale. Alice said cowboys were all right, but that the reason she bought the shirt was because the men's asses were all so cute. And also, mainly, because her initials were all over it. 'Your initials aren't A.S.,' I'd said. And she'd said, 'They used to be. Before I got married.'

I take a drink of my beer. It tastes too strong. I haven't had a beer since the night I got the call. I'd come home from the grocery store, late, after I'd been gone all day, and I'd started making dinner, and I was really tense because I knew it would never be ready on time and I cracked open a beer to calm down. I saw the answering machine flashing with a message when I sat the kids in front of the Mickey Mouse Club but I thought the hell with it and I started making the tomato sauce – eggplant parmesan, we were having. Once things had gotten going, I went in to pick up the message, told the kids to turn down the TV so I could hear. 'This is Dr Matthews at St Luke's hospital,' a too-calm voice said. And I remember I looked at the girls and thought, No, this is a mistake, they're right here. And then I thought about who wasn't here. 'You can turn the sound back up,' I told the girls when I finished writing down the number to call, and I went into the kitchen and turned off the sauce. Then I went into our bedroom and shut the door and I called

51

and while I was dialing I thought, Please just let him be alive I will do anything you want all the rest of my life if he is just alive. Then Dr Matthews came to the phone and I said yes over and over again. I believe that's all I said that whole conversation. I was holding the top button on my shirt so hard it left big dents in my finger.

'Alice?' I say now. 'I'm sorry. I don't like being here. I want to go home.'

'Give it a minute,' she says.

'What for? This is awful.'

'Do you know,' she says, 'that I never once got hit on? What's it feel like?'

I stare into my beer. 'You've been hit on.'

'What is that, are you being polite?'

I look at her to protest, but then say, 'Yeah. I suppose.'

'Well, don't be. I don't need that. I was never hit on, and that's that. Except once by a woman. You know how women have the good sense to look beyond looks.'

I start to say something, then realize the beer I've gulped is still in my mouth.

'What?' Alice asks.

I swallow. 'You never told me about that.'

'I never told you about that?'

'No!'

'Oh.' She takes a drink from her beer, stares straight ahead, taps her fingers in rhythm to the music from the jukebox.

'*So?*' I finally say.

'So what?'

'Come on, Alice.'

'Oh, it was no big deal. This woman was visiting another woman in my dorm, two doors down from me. We'd all heard about her, we knew she was a lesbian. She was gorgeous. One of those black-haired, blue-eyed types straight out of romance comic books. She was leaving and she walked past my open door and saw me playing my guitar and singing, and—'

'You play guitar?'

'Yeah.'

'You play *guitar*?'

'*Yes*. Quite well, in fact.'

'Well . . . Jesus, Alice. I didn't know that either. Why don't I ever hear you?'

'I don't play anymore.'

'Why not?'

'Oh, because Ed . . .' She stops, stares at me. 'Listen. Do you want to hear this story or not?'

'Yes!'

'All right then. So this woman pokes her head in and listens for a while and then she says, "Buffy Sainte-Marie, right?" and I say, "Right." She comes in and we start talking about Buffy Sainte-Marie and she asks me to play a few more songs and I do and then she says she loves music and the only thing she might like more is dancing and did I like dancing? I said it was all right. She said how about if I danced for her. I said I didn't think so. She said, Oh come on, she'd close the door, no one would see. I said I had to go somewhere.'

'And?' I say.

'And what?'

'And what happened?'

'Nothing. That was it.'

'That was it?'

'Disappointed?' Alice asks.

'I don't know. Yes. Of course.'

'Real life hardly ever does it the way you want to tell it later, Lainey.'

'I guess.'

'I should have done it. I've always been sorry I didn't do it. Now it's too late.'

'Why?'

'I don't know. You have a kid, you stop picking up hitchhikers. You know.'

I nod, stare at the rising bubbles in my glass. I'm a little drunk from just one beer. It makes things easier. I feel insulated from myself, a sympathetic bystander to my own predicament.

'So what *is* it like being hit on by a man?' Alice asks. 'Is it fun?'

'I was never hit on that much. I was never really into the whole bar thing. The closest I ever came was before I met Jay, when I dated this fraternity guy. He was like . . . You know what? He was like a wild pig. I swear to God. Like a big hairy boar. I don't know why I dated him except that he was in this big-deal fraternity, and my roommate was crazy about him. When he called me the first time she said, "Jake Laz*ar*? Oh my God, are you kidding? Jake Laz*ar*? Do you know who he *is*?" So I went out with him and we partied a lot and I always felt like I was doing exactly the wrong thing. I'd be putting on all this makeup and borrowing earrings and thinking, I don't even want to go. I don't want to do this at all. I thought I had to do it. I thought I'd never meet someone I could say the real things to. And . . .'

'Yeah? What?'

I don't say anything. I am thinking of something, caught up in a memory as though it had gained human form and pulled me up off the bar stool to hold my ear against its beating heart. Sometimes, when we were making love, I would put my fingers into Jay's mouth. It was not only for the eroticism of feeling the talented tongue, the warmth and softness and differing surfaces of that pink inside. It was to reach toward something. Once I rose up from where I had been lying on his chest, and pulled my fingers out of his mouth, used them to trace his lips with his own damp, then put them back inside his mouth. 'Open,' I said, and he smiled, a little embarrassed, but then he did open his mouth. 'No,' I said. 'More.' And when his mouth was as wide open as it could go, I put my own mouth over his. I wanted everything. I wanted to give everything, I wanted to take everything. We came so close it scared us. We had to laugh. We had to start giggling and get up and go into the kitchen. It was just after midnight. We made cinnamon toast and ate it quietly, so as not to wake the children. So as not to wake ourselves.

If he dies, and I am a young widow expected to date, what will I do? Come to places like this, where someone will say, 'So. Tell me about you'?

'Lainey?'

Well, there it is. I'm starting to cry. 'I can't be here, Alice,' I say, and I wipe my eyes quickly with the damp napkin from under my beer. 'I feel so . . . disloyal. I feel like I need to be paying attention all the time, just in case.'

'What? In case what?'

'Well, what do you *think*? In case of anything! What if they were calling me right now, saying he woke up?'

'Then Ed would call us here. And we're closer to Jay than we would be at home. By a good three blocks.'

'So we'd just go there right from here?' I say.

'Yes,' Alice answers softly, and I feel her compassion move out of her and settle on my shoulders like a coat.

I push my hands into my face, overwhelmed by the simple image of my husband walking in the door of the house where we live. 'I don't think I can stand up,' I say.

'You don't have to for a while,' Alice says. 'That's the idea.'

I have been there. How can I tell you this, other than to sit somewhere below you and look up at you, the sun all around me? What can I do but rock back and forth, my hands wrapped around my ankles, my face smiling, my eyes weeping, my throat closed and my heart stretched to the bursting? Say I drew the line in the dirt. Would you know to lower yourself to touch it?

56

Eleven o'clock. I don't know why I try to read. I can't make sense of anything. I turn off the light, close my eyes, sigh deeply. Like a waking dream, I imagine the ghost woman sitting on the bed beside me. She is in her nightgown, her hair loose about her face. 'Well now, what good does this do?' she says. 'This fretting. You've got to go right on and live your life, don't you see?' She smiles at me, leans forward and says in a low voice, 'He'll get better. It's just a matter of time.' Her voice is so strong, so real-sounding I shiver.

'How can you say that?' I ask. I hear my own voice, talking out loud.

'Well, you just have to,' she says. 'I don't know how you've all gotten so weak, you people now-adays. You think things are always going to be easy? You have to be strong!'

'Well, I'm *trying*,' I say.

She nods slowly, stares out the window. Then

she turns back to me and what is in her face is this: try harder.

I open my eyes, turn the light on, see nothing but the curtain moving in the slight breeze.

I know what this is. I've heard about things like this. You have a desperate need, you fill it in any way you can. You feel alone, you make someone up to be with you. That's all this is. It's harmless.

I go to look at the kids sleeping, check to see that the doors are locked, then get back in bed.

I startle awake, thinking I've overslept, but it's still night. The clock says 2:50, and then, as I watch it, the green numbers change to 2:51. I call the nursing home. The phone rings sixteen times before someone answers. 'This is Elaine Berman,' I say. 'I'm Jay Berman's wife. I was wondering if you could tell me how he is.'

A pause, and then a woman's lazy voice says, 'We have no one here by that name.' Then, before I can protest, 'Wait a minute. Hold on.' She puts her hand over the phone and I hear her ask someone if there's a John Berman here. Then, coming back to me, 'Oh. Sorry. Yeah, he's here. *Jay* Berman, right? And . . . what was the question?'

'I just . . . I wondered if he was doing all right.'

'Far as I know, he's fine.'

Tomorrow I will do whatever I can to have this woman fired. 'Could you just go and look at him? He's in the third room down on your right. 203.'

'He's not my patient.'

'Well, whose patient is he?'

'I believe he's Theresa's. I'm not sure. But she's on break.'

I sit up on the edge of the bed. Should I go down there? Or am I creating an emergency out of nothing?

'Please,' I say. 'Could you just go and look in his room and see if he's all right?'

She sighs. 'Hold on.'

I tap my heel against the floor, bite at my lips. Then I hear the woman – girl? – pick up the phone and say, 'He's fine. He's sound asleep.'

'He's in a coma,' I say.

'Oh,' she says. 'Sorry.'

'Yes.'

'But he's asleep anyway. You know. He didn't say nothing.'

Maybe later I'll laugh about this. Maybe when I tell Alice this later, we'll hold on to each other's arms, laughing, and she'll make that little wheezy sound she makes when she laughs hard, that always makes me laugh harder.

'Thank you,' I say. Unbelievably.

'Sleep,' I hear the ghost woman saying. 'For heaven's sake, go to sleep and stop this hysteria. You have children to care for in the morning. You have a husband to visit. That's enough to do.'

I am walking down the hall of the nursing home when I hear a voice behind me. ''Scuse me,' it says, and then, louder, ''*Scuse* me!' I turn to see a gigantic black man, squeezed into a wheelchair, attempting to get past me. He smiles, revealing king-sized dimples, then steers past me down the hall. He stops suddenly, yells into a room. 'Yo, Candy! I need some orange juice. You done fucked me up with that insulin. Get me some juice. Two packs of sugar.'

A weary-looking woman, fortyish, with half glasses on her nose, emerges from the room she was in. 'I hear you, Flozell. I'll get you some juice. And my name is Mrs Thompson, and you know it.'

'You be "Candy" today, darlin',' he says. And then, turning to wink at me, 'And *you* be . . . "Peaches"!' He looks me up and down with lascivious pleasure, readjusts his belt buckle. He wears a shoe on one foot, bandages on the other, shiny blue slacks, a white T-shirt and a gold necklace with a round medallion. Jay used to be wearing pants and a T-shirt, no shoes, when he came down for his second cup of coffee in the morning. The first cup, he'd bring in to keep him company while he shaved. His hair would still be wet. He'd smell so good, like soap.

I get to Jay's room, close the door behind me. I can hear the sound of the birds outside, and this seems such a sad thing.

'It's Sunday, Jay,' I tell him. 'It must be sixty out there. And the air is so soft!'

This suit is too loose, Lainey. Take it off. I am drowning in soft folds of dark. I am being pulled along, the air is so thick. Is it insects I hear? Violins?

'I guess spring is really here,' I say. I have his head raised about thirty degrees, and I have positioned pillows on either side to keep it from leaning. I've put his hands out on top of the covers to rest over his stomach in an arrangement of some normality, though he does have rolled-up washcloths in his hands to keep them from closing up too tightly. And of course his eyes are shut. Nobody would be fooled for a second.

But this is my new plan: I will attempt to make things around him as normal as possible. He used to like to watch the news shows while he was getting dressed in the morning, so I've taped a sign to the television: PLEASE TURN THIS ON TO THE TODAY SHOW FROM 7 TO 9 EVERY

61

MORNING. It's hard to say if they'll do it, but it's worth a try. I also want to dress him, to put different kinds of fabric against his skin. I brought a blue striped shirt today, maybe he'll smell something on it that will get him going. It was hard getting it on him. I was afraid I was hurting him when I put his arms through, but of course I couldn't tell. Gloria, the fat black nurse's aide taking care of him today, frowned when she saw the shirt. 'What's this?' she asked.

'It's a shirt he wears to work,' I said. 'I want him to wear things from his normal life.' I buttoned one of the tiny collar buttons that had come undone.

'Well, it's going to be in the way,' she said. 'I got to hook up his feeding tube right now. This shirt don't move out the way like the patient gowns do.'

I got up, raised his shirt. 'There,' I said. 'I'll hold it out of the way if you want.'

She scowled, hooked up the tubing, hung the bag on an IV pole. Then she opened the roller clamp, started the drip. She was wearing heart-shaped earrings that as far as I was concerned were lying. 'It's going to get all stained,' she said, 'I can tell you that. Big yellowish stain, it don't come out easy. And then you be all the time having to wash his shirts, carry them back and forth.'

'Yes, well,' I said. 'That's all right.' She had no idea what exquisite pleasure it would give me to pull his shirt from the dryer.

And so now I am telling him it's Sunday in my

normal voice, rolling the bottom covers up over his feet to put his favorite argyle socks on him. They don't exactly match his shirt, but they're his favorite. I've brought his favorite sneakers, too.

'It would be your turn to make the pancakes today,' I tell him. 'You actually make better ones than I do. You make that and Caesar salad better than I do, but that's all. Not that you couldn't improve. Maybe we should take a cooking class together. There's a good one at the Y, on vegetarian cooking, we should do more of that kind of eating. A lot of people do it. They say it's easy to get used to. There are much better recipes now than there used to be.'

I finish tying his sneakers, put the covers back over him. I don't want Gloria to see the shoes quite yet. I pull my chair close beside him, my back to the door, facing the window so that when I look up I can see the veil of new leaves on the tree outside. Hope. 'You remember when we first made Caesar salad?' I ask. 'You'd given me *The Joy of Cooking* for Christmas, remember? We'd just started living together. And we got stoned from the roach your friend Dave left behind, remember your friend Dave, who wanted to be a hippie and lived on a commune? Remember how he told us his girlfriend had a baby and they ate the placenta and buried the cord under a tree? God! Do you think they really did that? I don't think so. But anyway, we started looking at recipes and it seemed so impossible that there were *instructions* for making all these fabulous things, they weren't secret, they were in English, black and white, there you are, anyone could do it. Just go buy the stuff, do what Erma says, and there, you get to have Caesar salad! You have rack of lamb, prime rib, potatoes au gratin; you get to have chocolate *mousse*! We walked to the Red Owl on the corner, it was so cold that day, remember? The stuff in our noses froze. I remember we got anchovies which we'd never bought before and we got all the other stuff and then we came home and made the salad in a Dutch oven, because we didn't have a big enough bowl, and we didn't use forks, we just picked up those big romaine lettuce leaves and ate it like Erma said was the best way to do it and it was so *good*. And then we found the recipe for brownies and made those. That was the best meal I ever had, Jay. When you come home, we're going to do that again. Do you want to?'

I look at him. He's lost weight; his cheekbones are too visible. A crystal-clear line of drool has started down from the side of his mouth and I wipe it off with the sheet, I don't know where his Kleenex has gone to.

'Jay?' I say, aware of my own foolishness, feeling it like a wadded-up thing on the bottom of my stomach. 'Jay? Did you hear me?'

What I know now, I can never tell you back. Here are my hands, immersed in water they remember. Here are the stirrings of the elements. I can look in here, in the clearness, and see every atom, every spark. If I could pull this all in, carry it back with me to the other life, if I could sit out on the porch steps with you and start to talk the real language, we would only end up weeping, holding each other against the terrible beauty that is always our lives. We cannot say so much. We cannot even pretend to see it. We must live as though we don't know. We must keep the secret. This is the real curse that came from the Garden.

'Jay?' I say. Behind me, I hear someone approaching and I turn around to see Gloria.

'He can't hear you,' she says, a wise sorrow in her voice. 'He's in a coma. You know.'

I look down at my purse, wonder how much she heard of what I said to him. Then I say, 'Well, actually, people in comas can hear, Gloria. I'm surprised you don't know that.'

'Oh, that's what they say, I know that. But I never saw no evidence myself. I never saw people waking up, saying "Remember when you said this to me, remember when you said that to me?" Uh-uh.'

Here would be the obvious place for me to say, 'So . . . you do see people wake up, then? Here?' But I say nothing, watch as she squeezes the bag with Jay's feeding. It's almost gone, and she clamps the line, starts to remove the tubing.

'There's more in there,' I say.

'I beg your pardon?' She is fumbling with his shirt, frowning all over again.

'I said there is more in there. In the bag. Of his feeding.'

'There ain't but thirty cc's or so.'

'I would like him to have it, though.'

She turns to me, and I can see her deciding if it's worth arguing. Then, 'Fine,' she says. 'But I'll be busy now, and this thing will run out, and I won't be here to flush the tubing. And then the feeding tube'll get all stuffed up. That stuff turn to cement, you leave it there too long.'

'Well, I'll do it,' I say. 'I'll flush it.'

'You know how?'

A hand of fear, clutching the back of my neck. 'Just . . . I've seen it. You just use that big syringe, put some water in, right?'

'That's it.'

'I'll do it.'

She nods, leaves the room.

I don't know why I said that. I can't do that. What if I hurt something? That tube goes right into his stomach, which is some pink-colored, pouch-shaped thing, from what I recall from sixth-grade health. I think it's wrinkled on the inside, little ridges on the lining, or is that some other organ? I don't know. But I should know what the stomach looks like before I put things in it! I can't do this. I could put too much water in and hurt something, rupture it, whatever they say. I'll have to go get Gloria or someone else when the thing is empty. And now I'll have to watch the bag until everything is gone, which suddenly seems so hard. Sometimes I just talk too much.

When the bag looks like it's empty, I go out into the hall. I'll find Gloria, apologize, bring donuts in to her tomorrow, I happen to know she favors lemon-filled, powdered sugar on top.

I don't see any nurses in the hall, and so I start looking in rooms. Behind the third door is Flozell. He is sitting in bed with his chest bare, washing exuberantly under his arm from a blue plastic basin. I notice the fatherly smell of Old Spice. 'Well, looky here,' he says. 'There's my new girlfriend. How you doing, Peaches? You want to come on in here and help me?'

I close his door, and then I see Gloria coming down the hall. 'It's empty,' I say. 'And—'

'I know, I know,' she says, waving her arm, and walking quickly past me. 'I'll do it.' And then she mumbles some more things that I can't hear. But can certainly guess at.

She reaches the room before me and I hear her say, 'Who put the damn *sneakers* on him?'

'I did,' I say, coming into the room. I lean against the wall, watching her. 'I'll take them off.'

'Leave them on,' she says. 'They'll help prevent foot drop. That I *have* heard of.'

The kids are gone to a movie when I get home. Double-header matinee. Alice again. How will I ever, ever repay her? I step out of my shoes, leave them in the hallway, which I would yell at the kids for doing. There's a stack of letters from yesterday on the floor below the mail slot, which I now pick up and sort through. Bills. A car magazine for Jay, which makes my throat ache. A letter from my mother, which I open and read on the spot. She will have enclosed a check, which I can use. Yes. One hundred dollars. And on pretty floral stationery the usual stuff about what she'll put in her garden this year; how she has fallen behind in her housework, she's not as young as she used to be, don't we know *that*, ha ha. And then, 'You know that Dad and I are praying every day for Jay, and for you, too. We know everything will be just fine. Remember, if you want us to come, we will.'

I reread the letter, then throw it away. We live skimming, eating the small bugs off the surface. I will cover my children tonight. I will decide on the food they will eat. I will fold their small socks and put them back in their drawers. 'I love you,' I will say, and press their growing shapes into me. 'I love you,' I will say, and run my brainy finger down the oblique line of their shoulder blades, their old angel wings. This is as far as we are allowed to go. Inside, love roars louder than we can hear. Outside, we write letters that don't begin to say what we intend, and fold our children's socks.

I don't want my parents to come. I don't want Jay's parents to come anymore either. What can they do? Distract me from my sorrow when what I really need is to occasionally immerse myself in it? It's like a big hand pushing at me all the time. And sometimes I just need to give in to it, sit in the bathtub and cry hard. I don't do it when the kids are around. With them, I act as though everything is fine. Different. But fine. I'm glad they're not here now.

I go upstairs, turn on the tap, lay out a towel. I think the kids have some bubble bath in the linen closet, I'll use that, even though the scent is grape gum. When the tub has begun its slow fill – the water pressure in the bathroom is ridiculous, we never did find out why, or fix it – I go into the basement, sort some laundry. After my bath, I'll put a load of underwear in, make sure the girls are set with clothes for school on Monday. I upend the basket of dirty clothes, start pulling out what I want to wash.

'Can't get ahead for being behind,' I hear. 'Isn't it the truth?'

I drop what's in my hand, turn around. No one. Then, when I start sorting again, I see the ghost woman standing by the wringer, doing her own laundry. She is wearing a blue-and-white print dress, a floral apron over it. 'You don't have to worry about those stains on your husband's shirt,' she says. 'You just soak them in a little white vinegar and water first, the stain will come out fine.'

'My God, I am exhausted,' I say, to her, to my own unraveling self.

'Take a nap,' she says, straightening suddenly, as though she has a kink in her back. 'Twenty minutes, do you a world of good. I used to do that when the kids were little, take a nap right with them. It was awfully nice to pull down the shades in the middle of the day, slip off my shoes and lie on top of the spread. I'd wake up before the kids, go down into the kitchen and do a little for dinner, maybe peel the potatoes, or try a new dessert. I'd have the radio on low, I liked to listen to the afternoon shows. It always refreshed me so, to take a nap. Then when the kids got up, why, I was happy to see them again.' She hikes her basket up on her hip, juts her chin at me. 'Go ahead, take your bath and lie down.'

I see her so clearly, her left arm across her waist, helping to hold the basket. The tiny diamond on her wedding ring has turned to the side; the ring has gotten too big. I swear I can see her beating heart in her throat. And I know about her. She uses dark-blue ink in her fountain pen, signs her letters, 'As always.' She takes her slippers off at her side of the bed at night, leaves them lined up and ready for when the morning sun pushes into her bedroom. She drinks from jelly glasses washed in the metal dishpan, rinsed in water that reddens her hands, then dried with a dishcloth embroidered with pastel daisies. She feeds her children lunch at a table covered with decorated oilcloth: sandwiches cut on the diagonal, milk; and on Friday, a Baby Ruth for dessert. She uses cold cream from the five-and-dime that comes in a white jar with a pink top. She prays on her knees at night, her head bowed, her faith steadfast and unquestioned. She has never looked at herself naked. Her back bothers her frequently, but she doesn't mention it.

I mean, I could just go on and on. It's like idly looking down into a well you thought was dry and seeing the black face of water so obviously deep you feel fear in the pit of your stomach like a fist.

It is worrisome, what is happening to me. As though there weren't enough going on. I'm just tired. I'm just too tired. I do need a nap. My subconscious has had to grow big, has had to play tricks to get me to pay attention to my most basic needs. I turn out the basement light, then turn it back on, head upstairs on legs that feel like they have the flu.

*   *   *

I sleep awhile, a good half hour, and then wake up
with a fuzzy-brain feeling. I go to the bathroom
and splash my face with cold water, then go
across the hall to Sarah's room, sit on her bed,
think about what we should do for dinner tonight.
We always used to order out Chinese on Sunday
night – shrimp with lobster sauce, he got that
every time – then eat in front of a rented movie. I
haven't done it since the accident. I wanted to wait
for him to be back. But maybe we should just start
doing things again, without him.

I lean back on my elbows, feel a lump on the
bed, turn and reach under the covers to take it out.
It could be anything: a shoe, her lunchbox, a book
she is reading. It is a book, her diary, a white
leather thing, gold trim, unlocked. I know I
shouldn't, but I open it and read the last entry.

*I think my Dad is dead. I told Lindsey, but that's
all.*

Oh, Sarah, I think. Do you really believe I
wouldn't tell you? But the truth is, I keep so much
from her. Surely she knows that; kids are all the
time being smart in ways you wish they wouldn't
be. Just learn your math, we think; never mind the
secret places in your parents' hearts. But they
know when you're hiding something. Why
should she not think I'm hiding the fact that he's
dead? Why should she believe he's alive when he
lies unresponsive to her every word, when he no
longer rolls up his sleeves to help her make Lego
cities, when he no longer checks her homework

and tells her she's a genius, or lies on her bedroom floor with his hands behind his head, his ankles crossed, listening to all she wants to say before she goes to sleep?

I put the diary back under her covers. Then I go into my bedroom, stare at his side of the bed. There's a wrinkle there. I go over to straighten it out, but I don't just give a little tug. I pull a bunch of fabric into my fists, and then I start shaking it. 'You're so stupid,' I say. 'Walking under ice. What's the matter with you?' I pull the spread off the bed, throw it onto the floor. Then I pull off the sheets and I hear myself making the growling noises I used to make when I played monster with the kids. 'Stupid!' I say. 'You never think of anyone but yourself!' I stomp all over the sheets, try to rip them, fail, try again, succeed. I tear both sheets into long shreds. Then I walk over to the dresser and upend his top drawer, watch the rain of boxers and T-shirts and folded socks. 'Now what do I do?' I ask them. 'Huh? Now what do I do? You tell me! You tell me!' And then, of course, I start sobbing. I sit down on the floor, hold one of his T-shirts against me and ask him to forgive me. I say I am just so scared.

I cry until my stomach aches, until my throat is sore. And then I get up and put Jay's things away, put fresh sheets on the bed, carry the torn ones out to the trash.

Tonight I will try once again to teach Sarah how to use chopsticks. And then I will start being honest. 'Sarah,' I will say, looking her right in the

73

eye, my insides true and calm as a ticking clock. 'Daddy is in a coma, and I still hope he will wake up. I still believe he will wake up. I know you said you don't want to see him anymore, but I think we should all go together next time.' And then I will take her to see him, which frightens her, I know, Amy too; but I will take them to see him and I will say, 'Talk. He can hear you. That I know. I really do know that.'

And if I need to cry, I will cry. 'I'm just feeling sad right now,' I'll say. 'I just need to cry to feel better. Maybe you need to, too. It's all right.' What would be wrong with that? What would be wrong with the three of us sitting on the sofa in the living room, crying together? The three of us asking together in silence for something we want too much to say out loud. There is nothing wrong with that. It's probably only real prayer.

I want to get up. This long, bright field of things waving, you are all on the other side. The field is so bright, yellow sun, and then a rush of birds rising up, their calls, their calls to me, three birds. They rush toward my face and then they are gone, black dots high up in the sky, shimmering pepper.

I work at a beverage distribution center. Beverage World, it's called. I can walk to it. There's a globe on a pole outside the small brick building. It used to spin on its metal axis. Now it stays still, rusting a little more each day. There's a big office with two desks in the front; a smaller room in the back where the boss, Frank, sits. He's one of the most elegant-looking men I ever saw: tall and slender; neat mustache; thick, gorgeous gray hair; looks like he ought to rule a country or at least conduct symphonies. He loves sailing, has little toy boats all over his office and one of those wave-in-glass things that offer an approximation of the continuous comfort of the ocean. He has a terrible stutter. You just don't know what to do, sometimes, when he gets going. You just stand there, thinking really hard *it's all right, you just take your time, I'm not mad, don't worry* but of course he does worry, he feels really badly that he just can't spit it out. He's a nice man, he lets me come and go, work around the kids' schedules, leave early if I need to, come in on Saturday if I want to. The woman I work with in the front, Dolly, is in love with him. She's full-time, she's worked with Frank for twenty-three years, and I don't think he knows how she feels. He's married, happily; Dolly's shy and careful. She wears, with no sense of irony, pearl-decorated glasses chains and cardigan sweaters buttoned at the top. She's so happy when Frank's on the phone and can't get his own coffee. She carries it in to him as though it's her heart on a silver platter, which of course it is.

It's not a glamorous job, by any means, but it's a break from the house and a little extra income that I've been saving for the kids' college tuition. I'm the girl Friday: I do a little filing, a little phone-answering, even a little bookkeeping, though that terrifies me. I get to pay bills sometimes; I really like, for some reason, paying the trucking companies. They have solid, reliable-sounding names – Indianhead, TransAmerica – and I like the associated images I always get: fat guys climbing out of big black trucks named Rita and going in for a plate of meat loaf and mashed potatoes and green beans, leaning back and picking their teeth afterward, satisfied as Romans after a banquet. Or young, slim guys with Elvis sideburns and cowboy boots drinking coffee straight from the thermos and driving far into the night, the only vehicle on the road. I see them cranking up the country-and-western, singing along a little, looking for company on the CB, watching the night-softened horizon out the left-hand window like a miles-long floor show. I understand there's a fair number of female truckers now, and sometimes I get a notion that in another life, that would have been the job for me. Just keep moving, you know. Socialization at the counters of the restaurants. 'Okay, June, how about some of those blueberry cakes?' I'd ask the waitress I knew pretty well just outside Toledo. Her with her forty-year-old ponytail, her fading sexiness, nice mole above her upper lip. 'How's the ride today, Lainey?' she'd ask, wiping down the counter beside me after she delivered my order. 'Hear you just come out of some heavy rain.'

'Yeah, it was going pretty good there for a while,' I'd say. My king-sized windshield wipers would have been thunking out a heavy rhythm that was still in my brain. June would tell me about the P.I.E. guy she had a one-nighter with and I'd say, Now June that's dangerous for your body and your spirit and she'd say, Oh, she knew that, but what the hell, he untied her apron when she poured his coffee and smiled up at her with those dimples – Lord! What was she supposed to do? Sit home alone in her bathrobe looking at reruns? Not this girl. She wasn't the stay-at-home type, not yet. She'd make a giddy-up sound, wink at me, then go to pick up the order for chicken-fried steak the cook in the back was yelling about. 'Aw, hold your horses, Mikey,' she'd say. 'Settle down back there, you're gonna blow a gasket.'

I called work a few day ago to say I still couldn't come in and Frank said that was perfectly all right, not to worry; he said they had a temporary worker, driving Dolly nuts with her gum-chewing, but otherwise doing just fine. I should take my time, come back whenever I was ready. And . . . how was he?

'Oh,' I'd said. 'No change.'

'I'm so s-s-s-s-s-s-s . . . regretful,' Frank said.

'Thank you,' I said. The sound of his voice made me wish so hard to be sitting there at my desk, making out the grocery list before I left for home and a normal evening, like I used to.

Monday evening, the setting sun coloring the clouds pink as cotton candy. The kids and I are on the way to see him. We've brought offerings: from Amy, a drawing of stick-fingered, smiling people, a family lined up outside a house with heart-shaped window boxes. The woman wears a blue triangular skirt, the man rectangular brown pants. There are two little children, a boy and a girl, dressed identically to their parents. Sarah has made a tape of herself reading some of *The Secret Garden*, her current favorite. I have brought an embroidered pillowcase that my grandmother did years ago, and Jay's Weejuns, and some apple crisp which I know he can't eat but which I want to heat up in the microwave and put under his nose. I'm a little nervous. I've prepared the girls for the patients in the nursing home, but they still might stand stock-still when we walk in, stare at one of the residents, feel fear knocking about inside them. Maybe they'll sit down on the floor and say, 'No!' like when they were toddlers and didn't want to put their jackets on.

'He has his own room,' I say now, looking in the rearview mirror at the two of them sitting together in the back seat. Usually they fight over the front seat, but tonight they both wanted to sit back there.

'You already said,' Sarah says.

'Oh. Yes. I did. Right.'

'Look!' Amy says, pointing out the window. 'Dairy Queen! Can we bring him some ice cream?'

'He can't eat it, honey.'

'Well, you're bringing him apple crisp.'

'Yes, but for the smell.'

'Ice cream has a smell. He likes Dairy Queen the best. Butterscotch sundae. That has a smell.'

I turn on the blinker. Fine. I'll go back, get him a sundae. We can put it on top of the apple crisp. It's sort of crazy, but I'm starting to get excited. *'Ice cream woke him up?'* Alice will say. *'Yes!'* I'll answer. 'And you know, it was Amy who suggested it, and I almost didn't stop!'

There is no one in the hall when we go into the nursing home. It is eerily quiet. 'Is anyone here?' Sarah asks. 'Is this the right place?'

And then, as though on cue, we hear the thin, high sound of an old woman's voice. I believe she is crying, but it is the thin, wailing variety, sorrow that expects no answer to its request, no relief.

'What's *that*?' Amy asks, stopping in her tracks. This is what I was afraid of. They will see all the human misery and it will kill them that their father is here.

'It's just one of the patients,' I say. Actually I'm pretty sure I know who it is. 'That's Mrs Eliot. She's really, really old and sometimes she gets upset and cries but then the nurses go in and she stops right away.' Not quite true, but a necessary lie at this time.

'Oh.' Amy starts walking again. 'I thought it was a ghost.'

'There are no ghosts,' I say. 'You know that.'

'Well, my word,' she says in my head. 'Deny me twice more, why don't you?'

'Here's his room,' I say, outside Jay's door. 'Are you ready?'

They nod, together.

I push open the door. He is on his side, pillows at his back to hold him over. He is turned away from us. 'It's me, Jay,' I call out. 'And Amy and Sarah are here, too.' I have the absurdly hopeful thought that he will say, 'Oh, well in *that* case!' and sit up, fling the pillows aside, ask for a drink of water, and then, a little embarrassed, push at the pieces of hair that stick out from the side of his head. He will feel something weird, lift up the sheet a little, look down at the cathcter in his penis and say, 'What the hell is this, Lainey? Go see if you can get someone to get this thing off me.' And I will say, 'You girls stay here with Dad. I'm going to go tell them he's awake.' And then, 'See?' I will say. 'You see?'

Of course Jay doesn't do that. His door swings

81

closed behind us, and we walk slowly around to the other side of the bed, stare at him. His eyelashes are so long and beautiful. The kids got them. Sarah is hanging back against the wall, but Amy goes up to Jay, touches his hand, says softly in her breathy child's voice, 'Hi, Daddy.'

Then, looking up at me, 'Can he really hear me?' I nod.

'Hi, Daddy,' she says again, a little louder. 'I brought you a drawing. Of a family.'

'Is he cold?' Sarah asks.

'No, I'm sure he's fine,' I say. 'He has a blanket on, see?'

'No, I mean, his hand. Is his hand cold?'

'No,' Amy says. 'Here. Feel it.' She steps aside and Sarah comes forward, reaches her small hand through the bars. At first, it lies across his; then she slides her fingers into the familiar pocket of his palm. She takes a big breath in, sighs out. Then, 'Mom? Can we be with him by ourselves?'

'You mean . . . you want to be alone with him?'

'Yeah. Right, Amy?'

'Yeah!' she says. And then, '. . . I guess so.'

'All right,' I say, and I have to think very hard about whether or not to add, 'Don't hurt him.' I decide not to. I decide to just stay close. Who knows what made Sarah ask for this? It is so mysterious, I feel I ought to honor it. I get the apple crisp and the ice cream to take with me. The room with the microwave is right next door. I'll be able to hear if anything goes wrong.

I put a paper towel on the bottom of the

82

microwave, really, the thing is filthy, they should clean it. Maybe I'll clean it. I set the timer for a minute and a half, lean against the counter far away from the thing so I'm safe from whatever a microwave does to you, I forget exactly what it is. Who can keep up with what we've done to ourselves, the invisible dangers in a normal day wrought by overactive technology, fueled by greed. Soon we'll have a whole world meeting for the purpose of saying, 'Oops. What should we do?'

Just as the timer rings, a man comes into the kitchen. We startle each other, my hand goes flying up to my throat. This is something I've done involuntarily since I was a little girl: I get scared, my hand goes to my throat and I squeeze it a little. The more frightened I am, the harder I squeeze. One of these days I'm going to strangle myself.

'I'm sorry,' the man says. 'I didn't know anyone was in here.' He's very handsome, dark hair and eyes, tall; vaguely reminiscent of someone famous, though I can't think who. He's wearing a beautiful sweater. Expensive, you can tell.

'It's okay,' I say. 'I'm done. I was just heating something up.' I take the apple crisp out, pour the nearly melted ice cream over it.

'Boy, that smells great,' the man says, and I must admit he is right. I put extra butter and spices in with the apples.

'Is that for . . .'

'It's for my husband,' I say. 'Not that he can eat it. He's . . . well, he's in a coma.' I smile, ridiculously. 'I just wanted his room to smell nice. You know. Well, actually, I hoped the smell would get through to him, somehow.' It drives Jay crazy, the way I do this, the way I am always giving more information than I have to. Say I stop at a toll-booth and ask directions. I can't just say, 'How do you get to Route 3A?' I have to say, 'Hi. We're going to visit a friend who used to be our neighbor and we got caught in traffic a while back so we're running late, and we'd like to find the fastest way to get there and another friend of mine told me 3A is actually better than the highway. But he's not the most reliable source. You know. So I thought I'd better check.' Jay says, Don't give more information than people need to know. But I always do anyway.

'He's in a coma?' the man in the kitchen with me asks now.

I look down. 'Yes, well . . .'

'My wife is in a coma, too.'

I look up quickly, wonder if this is a terrible, terrible joke, see that it is not. Oh, it is not.

He shrugs. 'Small world, huh?'

I nod. I feel a little sick.

'There's three people here in comas,' the man says. 'The other one, lady called Mrs McGovern, she's in her eighties. Stroke. Jeannie, my wife, she's . . .' He swallows against his pain. 'She's thirty-three.' He nods, pushes his hands into his pockets. There, in his balled-up fists, is his aching heart.

'I'm so sorry,' I say. 'Of course I understand

completely what you're going through. How long?'

He looks away, thinks. 'Six months. God. I'd forgotten.'

Six months! 'Three for me.'

He nods again.

'How did she . . .'

'Aneurysm,' the man says. 'She came into the living room after dinner one night, holding her forehead, and she sat down and she had this strange look on her face. She said she had a real bad headache. After just a few minutes, it was much worse and she said maybe we should call a doctor. So I took her to the emergency room and they admitted her to the hospital right away, they were going to do surgery the next day. During the night she lost consciousness. They did the surgery but she never . . . she hasn't woken up yet. She hemorrhaged in the OR, she arrested a few times . . .' He looks away, then back at me.

'I'm Lainey Berman,' I say, finally.

'Ted Nichols.'

'I'm so sorry.'

'Me too. For you, I mean.'

'Thank you. Listen, I have to get back to my children. They're with their father. I don't want to leave them alone too long.'

'Right. Well, we're in 222.'

'203.' I smile, back out of the room.

Out into the hall, I stand still for a minute, try to take in what I've just heard. Down at the other end of the hall, I see Flozell wheeling along behind

85

a woman who is painstakingly taking herself for a ride in her wheelchair. 'Get along now, Mary,' he is saying. Well, actually kind of yelling. 'I got to go faster than this. Let me by.'

'I certainly will not,' the old lady says, barely turning around. She is dressed in a brown-and-white polka-dot housedress and blue plastic slippers, nylons rolled to the knee. Her thin white hair is neatly styled into a French twist. She is wearing huge clip-on earrings, a pearl-and-rhinestone arrangement. The left one hangs down too low, nearly off her ear. 'You can just wait for me,' she says. Then, in a lower voice, but one he can still hear, 'I declare, you are the rudest man I have ever met.'

Flozell sees the apple crisp in my hand, stops before me. 'What you'd bring me, darlin'?'

I ignore him, start to walk away. A nurse comes up to him, sullenly offers him a cup of pills. 'I have been looking everywhere for you, Flozell,' she says. 'You know when it's time for your medication. I'd appreciate it if you would stay in your room at those times. I can't be running all over the place looking for you. I have too much to do. You ought to know that.'

'Lord, listen to you run on at the mouth,' he says, snatching the pills from her, upending the cup over his mouth, swallowing them without water. 'Run on at the *mouth*! I guess every woman in this place done got her period at the same time. You *all* cranky! Oowee! Man could *drown* in the female hormones 'round here, you girls vicious!'

'You hush up!' Mary says, then wheels herself serenely around the corner.

When I push open the door to Jay's room, I see Amy and Sarah stretched out on his bed, one on either side of him. They have removed their shoes; I see them neatly lined up on the floor by the dresser. On the outside I smile at this deeply familiar sight of him, a daughter on each side as though she grows there; and on the inside my heart breaks in half, one side falling neatly away from the other. I do things to help, and they hurt. I do things to hurt, and they help.

It's midnight, and Alice's dog Maggie and I are rocking again, though we are on the sofa this time, not in the rocker by the window. She has actually fallen asleep; I can hear her damp snoring. I am thinking about the man named Ted and his wife Jeannie. I still can't think who he reminds me of. Maybe nobody. Maybe he's just the kind of person who's good-looking enough that you think he ought to look like someone famous. I'll bet people come up to him all the time saying, 'Are you . . .?' And he has to all the time say, 'No.' I wonder what his wife looks like, what kind of couple they made. And then I think about all the other people there must be who have loved ones in a coma, who live in a state of desperate hope, not knowing what's going to happen, not knowing, not knowing, not knowing. And then, because I just can't think about this anymore, I turn on the television. I flip through the channels until I see Lucy saying, 'Awwwww, *Ricky*!' and then I sit back to watch. I hope Lucy calls Ethel on the phone. Every time she calls Ethel on the phone, it's a good one.

Maggie is actually getting a little heavy. I shift her over to my other shoulder. This wakes her up, and she pushes away from me, walks stiff-legged along the sofa to the end of it, lies back down. She puts her chin on her paws, sighs loudly through her nose.

'Well, pardon me,' I say.

Her ears twitch.

'You want some baloney?' I ask.

She raises her head, looks at me.

'Baloney?' I say.

She cocks her head, actually looks cute.

I go into the kitchen, peel off a slice of baloney, bring it out to her all rolled up.

'Don't get it on the sofa,' I say.

She eats it in one bite, looks to me for more. 'Forget it,' I say. 'But maybe later we'll have popcorn.'

She barks.

'Yeah, all right. Whatever you said.'

'Course, we never watched television,' the ghost woman says. She is standing in the corner, opposite the set, in her faded red chenille robe and white nightgown and slippers, hair in a braid over her shoulder. 'Didn't have one till after the kids were gone. We used to play cards a lot: gin rummy, canasta, poker, too – just for pennies. We'd set up the card table, invite the neighbors over, or my husband and I would just play ourselves. We did a lot of gabbing, laughing. When other folks were over, somebody would always run to Dixie Cream for donuts, bring back a whole box of them and then of course we'd have to make a pot of coffee. The kids played out on the porch, all rough-and-tumble, somebody was forever coming in crying, but then they'd want to go right back out there. Worst thing that ever happened is the night little Billy Ellerby got smacked in the head with the porch swing – we had a big white porch swing out there, lovely to sit in and watch the world go by. Well, he got seven stitches and you'd have thought he'd been elected king of the universe. Other kids couldn't get enough of looking at them, standing up close and staring at them till they got the willies; then they'd run away, and then they'd come back and do it all over again. He charged a quarter to feel them, never mind that he could have gotten a terrible infection, you'd have to practically call out the reserves to get any of those kids to wash their hands before dinner. But he charged a quarter and darned if he didn't earn enough money to buy the supplies he needed to make a go-cart. Built it right out in the backyard, entered it in a contest at the State Fair that summer and won himself a blue ribbon.'

I rub my eyes, sigh. I'm not much bothered by this anymore. I'm used to it. It's my odd comfort, listening to simple stories about a simpler life. I look back at the TV screen – Lucy *is* calling Ethel on the phone! – and when I look back, the ghost lady is gone.

At the commercial, I get up, stretch, yawn. I ought to go to bed. I turn off the TV, look out the window at the moon, draw comfort from its presence. I call Maggie, let her out the front door onto the porch, then outside. She'll stay in the yard, sleep behind the rosebushes. Alice and Ed let her run free, I really like that. She doesn't even have a collar.

I close the door to the porch, then walk to the end of it, look up at the ceiling. There, where I knew they would be, I see the marks from the hooks that held up the swing. And it comes to me as naturally as taking the next breath what her name was: Evelyn Arlene Benson, called Evie. And then I understand that there is an explanation for all of this. I remember that after I first moved in Alice and I found some old pictures of the house in the basement. Surely there must have been a photo of the porch swing. There must have been some old letters, too. I probably read them and then forgot about them. I must have. I do that sometimes, forget about things. Jay used to get mad at me for that. I would forget things he told me. 'Why don't you pay *attention* when I talk to you?' he'd say. 'What is it that you're *thinking* about all the time?' And of course I'd say I didn't remember. I close the front door to my house, lock it, dead bolt and chain.

I awaken to the sight of my younger daughter beside my bed. The clock says 1:50. Amy is making little snuffling noises, crying, her hands held together before her and caved in a little, as though in lazy prayer. 'What?' I say sleepily, hold out my arms to her. 'What's wrong, sweetie?'

She climbs into bed with me, turns onto her side, pushes her butt into my stomach and her thumb into her mouth. 'I had a bad dream,' she says.

'You had a bad dream?' I say. 'Is that what you said?'

She turns around, pulls her thumb out, studies my face. 'Yes. It was about a man who had no eyeballs. It was all white in there where his eyes go. He kept looking at me, though.'

'That must have been really scary.'

'Yes.'

'But you know it was only a dream.'

A pause, and then, 'Yes.'

'Would you like to stay here and sleep?'

'Yes.'

'All right.'

She turns away again, and her breathing changes within a minute; she's back asleep. The man she dreamed of had eyes that were all white, but he could see her. It's Jay she was dreaming of. He seems blind to us, but he sees. That must be it. This dream is the fragile intervention I need to keep up my faith. Not tearing up sheets. Why did I think that that kind of acting out was going to get me somewhere? If I lie on the floor kicking and screaming, who will be moved? The hard and constant lesson is that we are only observers here.

We do not move the pieces. We do not chart the course. We have our little parameters, like an insect captured in a shoebox. We strut back and forth, arranging and rearranging the arbitrary layout of the grasses we've been given. But with all the head-nodding we do, all the lip-smacking, all the self-satisfied pats to our overfull bellies, all the putting forth of what is really only speculation from our beginning brains, we aren't aware at all of the thing that is before us. Jay and I used to talk about this, how something superior must be so amused. Inside the box, we arrange and re-arrange. We plan and plan. We are so foolish, but we can't help ourselves. The shoebox seems so much to us. We plan and plan.

I get out of bed quietly, go to look at Amy's sheets. Yup. I take them off her bed, put them out in the hall. Tomorrow is soon enough to wash them.

After the kids go to school in the morning, I put Amy's sheets in the wash, then get back into bed. I'm too tired to go and see him. I need some rest, or I'll fall apart. Just after I go back to sleep, the doorbell rings. I punch the pillow, punch it again, harder. Meter man, I'll bet.

I yank open the door, annoyance all over me, and stare out at nothing. Then I look down and see Timothy looking up at me.

'What are you doing here?' I say. 'You'll be late for school.'

'That's secondary,' he says.

'Uh-huh. Well, what's primary?'

'What do you mean?'

'I mean, you know, why are you here?'

'My mom's sick. She needs a thermometer. We can't find ours. Do you have one?'

I open the door wider. 'Come in, sure. I've got one. I'll get it for you.'

He follows me to the bathroom, and I find a thermometer in the medicine chest, hand it to him. 'Should I come with you?' I ask.

He shrugs. 'Up to you.'

We cross the porch to their side, go into their house, and I see Alice lying on the living-room sofa. I sit beside her and before I can say anything, she says, 'What's wrong with you? You look like shit.' Then, to Timothy, 'You didn't hear that. I think you'd better go on, honey, I'll be fine.'

He looks at me. 'Go,' I say. 'I'll be here.' I say this, and I mean it, and I want to do it; but I am also thinking, Oh God, oh no, I want to sleep, and then I need to go see Jay. But I'll go tonight when Ed gets home. I'll do the day shift with Alice, the night shift with Jay. The edges of my stomach ache.

But then I look at the circles under Alice's eyes, her wan color. I love her. Someday I should tell her. '*I* look like shit?' I say. 'You ought to see you.'

'I know,' she says. 'I've been puking. I'm sorry.'

'You're "sorry." For God's sake, Alice.'

She smiles. 'No. You know. I can't watch your kids this afternoon.'

'Oh dear. I'll have to fire you.' She starts to say something and I say, 'Alice. *Thanks* for getting sick. Thanks for letting me do a little something in return. What *can* I do, by the way? Should I stay here?'

She thinks about it, then says, 'No. I'm loaded up on medicine, I think I'll sleep for a while. If you could just bring me the phone. I'll call you if I need anything.'

'Are you going to take your temperature? You look kind of flushed.'

'Oh, yeah, right,' she says, and slides the thermometer under her tongue. The mean thought comes to me that now I'll have to get another one what with the way no family wants another family's germs. Then I think how terrible I am to think that and that no one else would. I go to get their portable phone, which is in their bedroom.

The bed is unmade, a stain in the center of the sheet. I know what from. I lay my hand across my stomach, stare at the stain. It occurs to me that I'd forgotten all about that. I try to remember the last time; then, thinking it is too dangerous to do that, I go back downstairs, hand Alice the phone. She puts it beside her, then pulls the thermometer out of her mouth. 'Yikes.'

'What is it?'

'A hundred and two point six.'

'Are you serious?'

She nods, a cross between pissed and sorrowful.

'Want me to take you to the doctor?'

'Not unless it turns into a hundred and two point six.'

'You're sure?'

'Yeah, it's the flu. It's just the damn flu. Just put a pan with some water in it beside me here. My mom always did that with us when we were kids. If you were sick, you got to lie on the living-room sofa with a pan of water to puke in. It was only for puking, thank God, imagine how we'd have felt if she'd have mashed potatoes in it the next day. Anyway, if I have to puke and don't think I can make it to the bathroom, I'll do it in there. Then I'll call you to empty it, aren't you lucky?'

'I don't mind, Alice, I really don't. Please. Don't worry. Just get better.'

'I'm telling you, you don't look so hot yourself. Honestly.'

'I'm just tired.'

'Okay.'

'Want me to turn the TV on for you?'

'God, no. Then I'll puke for sure. No, I'll just sleep. I usually get over these things really fast. I'll be all right.'

Back at home, I sit in my kitchen, listening to the birds. I can't go back to sleep. I am so scared she has something bad. I am so scared she'll die, that's what it is. I don't know why this kind of thinking should surprise me. But it does. I twist the dish-towel in my hands for a good twenty minutes, asking for a calm that does not come and then I get dressed.

Here, at the back of my throat, a tickle. A cough? Winter and the snow falling in fat flakes, a silhouette before glass, fire. On my knee, a child sitting, my live hand on the back of her head, such fine yellow hair. The sound of your voice, Lainey, coming from the kitchen, sliding drawer, the bang of a pan. Silver, tinfoil stars, blunt-ended scissors, the first day of school. Mittens wet on the radiator, rippled air. A rustle of paper, the news on the television, steps walking across the carpet, those big shoes, my own father. Dad?

Ted and I are in the little break room at the nursing home. It's mostly used by the staff, but visitors can use it too. Ted is eating Cheez Doodles and drinking a Dr Pepper. I'm having a Nestlés Crunch. It's a celebration, because Alice did not die. No, did not die and felt fine the next day and showed me that not everything turns out crazy.

It's 7:30, dark outside; really, I should go home, but I saw Ted in the hall on the way out and it was clear he needed to talk.

He squeezes his empty bag into a cellophane ball, throws it across the room into the garbage, then asks. 'Do you ever feel guilty?'

I shrug. 'Sure. I mean, you know, about all the times I yelled at him, stuff like that?'

'No. What I mean is . . . do you ever feel like it was your fault?'

'Well, no. It was ice. It hit him in the head. I wasn't even there.'

'Right.'

'Why, do you, Ted? It wasn't your fault. She had an aneurysm! How could that be your fault?'

He nods, stares at the tiny table top, rubs at a stain with the flat of his fingers. He has graceful hands, like a pianist. He looks up at me. 'I think I made it worse, though. I think I made the vessel pop, or leak, or . . . something.'

'How could you have done that, Ted? You didn't do that.'

'Well, I . . . On the night she went into the hospital, they told her she had to stay in bed. But she wanted to go to the bathroom. I told her I'd go get a nurse to give her a bedpan. She said she didn't want to use a bedpan, she was afraid it would spill, she'd mess up the sheets. She didn't want to use a bedpan. She wanted to walk to the bathroom. So I thought, well, what the hell, I was there, wasn't I, I'd help her not to fall, I could even carry her back to her bed if I needed to, she didn't

99

weigh anything. But she did fine – I really didn't help her at all, just walked behind her. She had just gotten back in bed when the nurse came in, asked if she wanted to wash up a little before she went to sleep. She asked if she needed the bedpan. And we just sort of looked at each other, Jeannie and I, our little secret. And then the next day in surgery she hemorrhaged. See, I think maybe she shouldn't have gotten up. I think that might just have been too much. And you know . . .' He looks up at me, starts to speak, stops.

'Ted. It wasn't your fault.'

'How do I know that, Lainey? They told her to stay in bed. And then I just ignored them. I'm so fucking arrogant, sometimes; I think I don't have to follow rules. I think they're for someone else.'

He puts his hand over his forehead, then pulls it down across his face and when he looks up I see that his expression has changed. I used to play a game like that with the kids, where I'd run my hand down my face and change expressions each time: they liked to see my open-mouthed surprise turn into a wide smile or a crossed-eye crazy face. Ted has turned agony into composure. 'Well,' he says. 'Anyway.' He offers a downward smile, lips held tightly together to prevent trembling, the kind of smile that precedes an outburst of tears in women. And then, 'Would you like to see her?'

I look at my watch.

'It won't take long,' he says. 'I know you have to go. It'll just take a minute. She's not much of a talker lately.'

100

'Yes, all right,' I say. It's only fair. He's met my kids; he's peeked in at Jay; he's listened to plenty of my stories in the last couple of weeks.

I follow Ted down the hall to Jeannie's room, take a breath before I go in. The room is identical to Jay's, but in this bed lies a dark-haired woman, thin, clad in a blue hospital gown. She is lying on her side, sheet pulled up to her bony shoulder. Her hair is neatly combed back away from her forehead. Her rings are loose on her fingers. She has high cheekbones, a beautiful nose, lips devoid of color. Over the bed, a floral handkerchief is Scotch-taped to the wall. Its colors are dusty pinks and purples; lace is crocheted around the edges. Seeing me looking at it, Ted says, 'That's her lucky hanky. She's had it since she was a little girl. Her mother gave it to her to bring along on the first day of first grade, and she's used it ever since. She took it to tests all through school, to her job interviews. On the day we got married, she had it tucked into her dress. Up the sleeve, you know, like old ladies do.' He stares down at her, hands in his pockets, rocks back and forth on his feet. 'She was gifted in mathematics, a rare thing in a woman.' He looks up at me, to see if I'm offended, I presume.

'Uh-huh,' I say.

'I know you have to go.'

'Yes.' I really can't stand being here. Jeannie has the same kind of eyedrops on her bedside table that they use for Jay, the same kind of lotion. She has a turning chart on her door, just like Jay, to

101

assure that her positon gets changed every two hours. I can't stand knowing that this happens to other people, that coma might be a relatively common phenomenon, that the treatment is the same, no matter who the person is. I have a feeling that they are unlucky, Ted and Jeannie, and that I must not stay here or I will be unlucky too. I hate the blackness of my own self, sometimes, my awful selfishness.

'Well,' I say. 'So.' I turn, start walking to the door.

Ted walks with me, stops at the hallway. 'I guess I'll stay with her for a while longer.'

'Right. I'll see you next time.'

'Lainey?'

I turn around.

'There's this woman at work, you know, she's . . . attractive, and she keeps—'

'Ted.' I can't believe he would say this so close to Jeannie. I look over Ted's shoulder, see the rise of her hip under the covers. It comes to me that she never got to have children.

'I know. I'm sorry. I know you have to go.' A blush is creeping into his cheeks. He looks slapped.

'I'll see you later, Ted.'

I walk quickly down the hall, go back into Jay's room, kiss his forehead good night. I am thinking that if someone told me he would never, ever wake up, I would still not be unfaithful to him. I will never be unfaithful to him. Never. I am pressing my lips into his forehead saying this word inside myself like a mantra. Never, never, but a singsong counterpoint is saying, Yes, you would, yes, you would. I recall the time Ted checked under the hood of my car in the parking lot of the nursing home, looking for the source of a noise I'd noticed. I'd looked at the muscles in his back and felt a spasm of longing as involuntary as a hiccough. The body will separate itself from the mind, sometimes. The body will make demands. How will I feel if Jay stays like he is for three more months? Only this morning I lay with my hand against myself, my eyes closed, crying and working away, thinking, No, this is not it. This is not nearly enough.

I put my purse on the floor, lower the bed rail, sit beside him. It won't come to that. I am not without power; I have a squared-off place within this life to exercise what I've been given. I will wake him up by sheer force of will, by my will alone. I take his hand, uncurl his fingers and then hold them. 'Every day more flowers are out,' I tell him, in a voice barely above a whisper. Then, a little louder, 'Sometimes I just can't believe that they're real. I mean, they're so complicated, when you look at them. Their insides. It seems like there could just be dots of color outside and we'd be satisfied. You know, just little flat disks of color, like little plates. But not only do we get the color, we get the variety, and those complicated insides. Sometimes it reminds me of ears, those curls and kind of crevices, you know?' His breathing is quiet, steady. In a firm voice, loud enough to carry across the room, I say, 'Jay, I don't know what you need to hear. But I know you're going to come home with me. Don't be scared. I can feel you getting better, and you'll come home with me soon. I'm just going to keep on telling you. I'm just going to keep on talking, and you listen, all right? That's all you have to do, is listen. Tomorrow I'm bringing you a tape. You want some jazz?' I wait, absurdly. 'You want that Monk tape?' Another beat. I let go of his hand, check my watch, smooth my skirt. I think I might have been yelling. I speak quietly now, say, 'I've got to go home and bathe the kids, honey. They don't like to take baths together anymore. Sarah locks the door even though I tell her not to, scares me to death, what if she falls? But I guess she needs her privacy. Yesterday she told me she needs a bra, can you imagine? I remember when I wanted a bra, about that same age. I told my mother I needed one and she said, "Whatever for?" and I said, "Well, it hurts when I run." That's what my friend Sherry Fessman told me to say. My mother just laughed. But then she got me a training bra with a little pink rose in the middle. I thought it was beautiful. It smelled like baby powder, and it was real soft, but when I put it on it was incredibly uncomfortable because it was so tight. I didn't care. I was thrilled to wear it even though all the boys snapped it. It was so humiliating when they did that. I hope you didn't do that, Jay. I'm sure you didn't. Did you?' I look into his face, his calm flesh palette, and decide no, he never did.

I go to the window and close his curtains tighter, so that it will be stronger when they open to the light. I pick up my purse, put it on my shoulder. I could make this purse, if I wanted to. I could tan the leather, forge the metal to create the buckle on the strap. These are things that are done on the earth, and I can do them. It is only a matter of deciding. I walk over to Jay. Then, once again, I kiss him. On the forehead. On each cheek. On his chapped lips, which I will also cure.

Underneath stirring, wave after wave. The sleepy sliding sideways tilt. My shoulder bone, porous gray, line of pain. Spaces between rocks, soft openings, the cool blackness. Eyes blinking, yellow thereness. What is that? A slick flash forward. Muddy river bank, the weeping willow, swaying hanging long green sickle leaves – no. No. Hair. Wait, your lips. You!

Nine o'clock. Sarah is in her bed, bedside lamp on, engrossed in a new book that is lying against her raised knees. She won't break the spine of a book, even a cheap paperback. She cradles her books in her lap like she's found the Grail. I don't argue against such reverence. I think it's right. When I was her age and finished a book I liked, I used to pet it, stroke the front cover, then the back; and then I'd kiss it.

Sarah's book is one in a series about baby-sitters. Every time I've been in a bookstore on a Saturday I've seen girls her age reaching up into the shelves for one or another of those books, then sitting on the floor to flip through them, idly scratching their thighs or shoulders, or feeling with their bitten-nail hands along the edge of their sneakers. I like those girls best when their pony-tails are sloppy, when they wear glasses. They are such strong and interesting creatures, not yet in the compromising grasp of boy-pleasing. Even though she's only ten, I am poised for Sarah to start asking when she can wear lipstick, to start saying her nose is wrong. Jay used to worry about how he would deal with our girls going out with boys. 'My God, I'll have to kill the guy before they leave, just to be safe,' he said once. We were lying in bed with our eyes closed, seeing the future. But it bothered us to see the girls older. We opened our eyes, turned on the lights, came back to the relief of the present. Jay went downstairs and brought up a sliced peach on a saucer. 'Want some?' he'd asked, and I'd eaten more than my half. That was a hot night. Three fans were running, the sound of summer. The outside of the peach was like baby skin; the inside so sweet it was faintly obscene.

'It's five after nine,' I tell Sarah now. 'Bedtime.'

'In a minute,' she says. 'Let me finish this chapter.' She doesn't even look up.

It's an intriguing idea, a book series based on baby-sitting. Tremendous number of possibilities, what can happen when you baby-sit. Once when I was sitting, I snooped idly in the parents' room after the kids were in bed. In his top dresser drawer, I found Polaroids of her naked. Well, not entirely naked. She was wearing her glasses. She was sitting on their living-room floor on an afghan in front of the fireplace, with only her glasses on. They were black cat-eyes. I wondered why she kept them on. I felt weird around those people after that, didn't want to sit for them anymore. I thought if they were going to do something like take naked pictures at least they should do it right, have the woman take her glasses off. But mostly I just thought it was strange. It made something rise in my throat, thinking of it. The next time they called me to sit I said no, and the time after, and then they stopped calling. It was wrong. They were nice people. So he loved her body. So what. Jay wanted to take pictures of me, once. I said no. I said, What if we get in a car wreck and the kids find them? I was also thinking what is in the back of nearly every woman's mind nearly all the time: just let me lose five pounds, first. Now I wish we'd taken Polaroids of each other.

I tell Sarah she can finish reading the chapter. Tomorrow's Saturday, everybody can sleep late. Then I go into Amy's room to tuck her in, sit on the side of her bed. She's freshly bathed, her wet hair slicked back from her head. The area under her eyes is bruised-looking; she hasn't been sleeping well. It is an unsettling thing to see circles under a child's eyes.

'Can I have oatmeal with raisins for breakfast?' she asks.

'Yes.'

'Well, we don't have any raisins.'

'How do you know?'

'I wanted some before, and Alice looked but we don't have any.'

'I think we do. Alice probably didn't look in the cupboard over the refrigerator. I have spare things up there.'

Amy shrugs. 'I don't know.'

I hope those raisins are there. After Amy's asleep, I'll check the cupboard. And if we're out of raisins, I'll go to the twenty-four-hour store on the corner and get some. It'll take me five minutes, the girls will be all right alone. And then when Amy wakes up and wants breakfast I'll open the cupboard and say, 'Yes, here are the raisins. Just as I told you. See?'

'You know what?' Amy asks now, after a huge yawn.

I stretch out on the bed, put my head on the pillow beside her, give her fragrant cheek a kiss. What is that smell children carry? Soap, mixed with clean kid sweat. Life. 'What?' I answer. My jeans feel too tight. I unbutton them, slide down the zipper a little ways.

'Once I spent the night with Lizabeth Healey? And she was eating cereal? In the morning? And guess what, she found a bug in it!'

'Really?'

'Yes, it had about a million legs and she started crying. And you know her brother, Carson? He said it came from her head!'

'Well. That wasn't so nice.'

'No.' She flips her teddy bear's ear back and forth between her fingers. Then she puts her thumb in her mouth, talks around it. 'Can we go to that big playground tomorrow? Behind Miller School?'

'Yes. I think maybe we should do that before we visit Dad.'

I stand up, pull her covers up, turn off her bedside lamp. 'Good night, sweetie.'

'All right,' she says. It's rare for her to say good night. She doesn't like it, I don't know why. She is turning into herself in these little ways. She is like stepping into the garden every day, when you know something is new, different from the day before. That's how children are, growing up in front of you the way they do. Sometimes it's a barely noticeable thing, like a stem that's slightly taller. Sometimes it's a blossom that's burst forth, obvious as a Vegas showgirl. Wow, you think. I'd better not miss a day. I'd better be here.

I turn on the bedside lamp. Three A.M. The chair in the corner, empty. The extra quilt, fallen to the floor. The shadowy outline of my perfume bottles, still. And that is all. Well, what did I expect? That Jay would come out of the shadows, grinning at me and saying, 'You should have heard the noises you were making! Bad dream?' That then he would slide into bed beside me, kiss me, stare with sleepy affection into my eyes before his hand went to my breast? His eyes are beautiful. I loved to look into them. I felt sometimes as though I would like to climb through them, to be into him. I thought that way I could achieve the intimacy our lovemaking hinted at. I wanted more than we had. I tried to tell Jay about this, once. At first he was offended, thinking I was talking about his technique. And I said no, no, it's not that; it's that I love you so much and I just want to be *in* there. And he said yes, he understood that, but he didn't think it was possible. He asked me if I knew what the word *asymptote* meant. I said no. He said it was a mathematical term and I asked him if he were crazy asking me if I knew about that when he knew I got panicked if the person at the cash register said, 'You want to give me a nickel so I can give you back a dollar?' He said no, this was a kind of higher mathematics that he thought I could understand, because when you got into higher math it emulated the nature of human beings. That you could see longing in mathematics, and elegance, and grace. And then he showed me the configuration of an asymptote, the tangents and the curved lines, and the way that they came very, very close to touching, but never quite did. That you could follow them out to infinity and they would be so close, but they would never touch. I said yes, that's right, that is a human longing and it's not fair that we have it if we can't have it fulfilled. And he said that it wasn't unfair. That we lived with knowledge of a promise that later, later, all things would be returned to us. How much later, I asked, and he said, Oh, way later. But in the meantime, we had such fine compensation.

I get up, go into the bathroom, turn on the light and look at myself in the mirror. No change. No answer. Then I turn out the light and go into the hall, pad past the girls' rooms. Both of them are uncovered, their limbs wild. Well. It's not that cold. Let them be. I've gotten lax with child care, I suppose. I can't keep up with everything I should.

Just the other day Amy went to school with no underwear. I noticed when she came home and was sitting halfway up the stairs, looking at a book and waiting for dinner. 'Amy?' I said. 'Where's your underpants?' She lifted up her dress, looked, and shrugged. 'I forgot,' she said. I imagined her teacher noticing, then wondering together with the principal if they should send a letter home. And then last week, Sarah came into the bathroom while I was standing with a towel wrapped around me, putting on deodorant. 'Amy ate some of that, you know,' she said.

'What?'

'Amy ate deodorant.'

I looked at the top of the deodorant. I didn't see any marks. 'This?'

'No. Dad's. Aren't you going to do anything about it?'

I opened the medicine chest to look for Jay's deodorant. 'It's not there,' Sarah said. 'She threw it away. She didn't like it.'

'Oh, my God,' I said. And then I ran down the hall to look for Amy, found her sitting on her bed, pulling her socks on. 'Amy!' I said. 'Did you eat deodorant?'

'No!' she said. And then, spying Sarah behind me, 'Fine, I just tasted it.'

'For Christ's sake!' I yelled. 'It's probably poisonous!' Amy's eyes widened. I ran into my room to call poison control, and the two of them ran after me, sat on my bed on either side of me.

The calm but concerned woman who answered

113

wanted to know how long ago Amy had eaten the deodorant. 'When did you eat it?' I asked her, my hand over the receiver. My towel opened and fell, and I pulled it back up. I was thinking, What is the fastest thing to put on so I can get her to the hospital?

Amy looked at me, blinked. 'Huh?'

'How long ago did you eat it? Quick!'

She frowned, thinking.

'It doesn't have to be *exact*,' I said. 'About when? Early this morning? Just a few minutes ago?'

'No,' she said. 'It was . . . maybe was it Tuesday?'

'It was last *week*, Mom,' Sarah said.

I told the person on the phone that it was apparently a number of days ago and that Amy had only tasted it. The woman said she wouldn't worry about it. Right, I thought. As if I could prevent myself from thinking that Amy would suffer some unique kind of damage at some point in her life that would be all my fault. Once I was in the drugstore picking up a few things and when I got to the register to pay for them there was a man in front of me who'd seated his little girl, maybe two years old, on the counter directly before him. He was offering her nearly constant sips from a huge cup of water, smiling at her, but also crying, lifting his glasses to wipe tears away. Once when she took a particularly big drink, the man said, 'Oh, that's good, honey, that's so good,' and he kissed her cheek tenderly, once, twice, three times. The pharmacist came up and gave him a

114

plastic bag, saying, 'Here. You're going to need this.' Then the pharmacist told me to come to his register, I could pay for my things there. 'Is this an Ipecac situation?' I asked quietly. 'Yeah,' the pharmacist said. 'Pretty soon that little girl is going to be real unhappy with her daddy. She's going to be throwing up like crazy.' He told me how the man and his daughter had been out on a walk and she had eaten some berries and the father hadn't known what they were. So he'd called the poison control center and they'd told him to get his daughter to throw up and then bring the stuff in to them so they could look at it. I thought, that little girl won't be mad at her daddy. When she's done throwing up, she'll put her small arms around his neck and lay her head against his chest for comfort and that will make him feel even worse than he already does. He'll be looking at the back of her pink dress, at her little shoes bumping into his stomach; he will be caressing her silky hair, and he will be thinking, Oh I'm so sorry, I'm so sorry, I am too careless ever to have had you. I'd wanted to tell that man, 'Listen here, don't you worry. I've had my kids do things like that and nothing ever happened. They're fine.' Only my kids had never done anything like that. Until Amy ate Ban. The poison control center asked me for my name and address and they sent me a lot of information about how to be careful in the future. Don't let your kids eat poinsettias. That kind of stuff. Well, I'll try. I was relieved they hadn't sent someone to arrest me.

I go downstairs and turn on the kitchen light, notice that a fluorescent bulb is out. I have no idea what kind it is or how to change it. I start to get mad at Jay, then let it go. This happens sometimes, my getting mad at him. I envision him as though he's enjoying himself, lying in bed, having his back rubbed a few times a day by a variety of women, not having to clean behind the toilet or fill the car up with gas or listen to the kids fight.

I put some water in the tea kettle, go to sit at the kitchen table. And then I hear a sound, coming from outside. It's someone walking around on the porch. I get up, feel gooseflesh forming on my arms, put my hand to my throat. I can call Alice and Ed. I can call 911. I wait, paralyzed, and then the tea kettle whistles. I rush to shut the burner off, then stand there. It's quiet now. My chest hurts. I get the biggest butcher knife I own and tiptoe out into the dark living room. I go over to the window, look through it, then breathe out my relief. It's only Alice. I see her sitting hunched over on the top step. She's smoking a cigarette, her elbows on her knees. I go to get my tea, make her a mug too. 'Sleepytime,' it's called. Very funny. My heart rate must be 140.

She turns around, surprised, when I open the door. 'Did I wake you up? I'm sorry.'

I hand her a mug, and she nods her thanks. 'You didn't wake me,' I tell her. 'I was up. Couldn't sleep.'

'Me either. Obviously.'

'Don't you hate it when that happens?'

She puts out her cigarette, shakes her head. 'No. I always feel like there's a reason. I never feel tired the next day. I just go with it – get up for a while, then go back to bed. My dad was like that. I think he got up almost every night, just took stock of things, then went back to sleep. I liked that he did that. It made me feel safe. Plus I was always sort of hoping he was thinking of me, reviewing my excellent qualities, thinking how lucky he was that he had me and what he would like to buy me.'

'He *was* lucky to have you,' I say. 'Didn't he ever tell you that?'

She takes a sip of tea, looks up at me. 'Yes. He told me that a lot. That's what accounts for my extremely good mental health. For my *nice*ness. Aren't I nice, Lainey?' She pats the place beside her.

I sit down. I'm not sure about the edge I've just heard in her voice. I suppose she might be a little angry at me by now, tired of giving. Even in the best of friendships and even under the most dire circumstances, the One will at some point get tired of giving to the Other. She will sigh behind her sympathy, clench her fists behind her back. I understand that. 'You must be about worn out, helping me,' I say.

'It's not that,' Alice says. She looks over at me. 'It's not.'

'Okay.'

I wait, but she doesn't offer me more. I drink my tea, survey the line of black trees along our block. The leaves have come out a little more, you can

117

see some progress every day now. It's such a forgiving time. There's something vaguely religious about it. Soon the trees will meet in the middle of the street, forming a high canopy, which is another good thing about living here. On a hot summer day, you turn down our street and feel like you're entering a cool, green tunnel. And though you know it's not true, you believe no one else has this.

'You know, Alice,' I say, 'I'm positive Jay's going to wake up. I know it. It's just a matter of time. And when he does, I'm going away. I'm going on vacation. To Bermuda. And he can just stay home and try to do everything, like I'm doing now. He can see how he likes it.'

Alice stares straight ahead, nodding. 'Yeah. Be gone a good month or so. Don't call, either.'

'Oh, I'm not. I'm not going to call or send a postcard or one thing. He can just suffer.'

'Right.'

It is quiet then, and the two of us sit and hold our mugs, thinking our own thoughts. There's a very bright moon, a black cloud across it that looks like a floating negligee. Werewolf moon. Black-magic moon. I feel a slight breeze move up under my nightgown and I close my legs together, pull the fabric tighter around me, then push my face into my lap. 'I can't think that he's not going to come back.' My voice is muffled like we're playing a game. Like I'm counting to one hundred before I can find anyone. 'I have to act like there's no question that he's coming back.'

'I know, Laincy,' she says quietly. 'I know that.'

I raise my head, look at her. 'So that's what I do sometimes, I make up these fantasies, think about punishing him. I think about revenge! It's so stupid!'

'It's not stupid,' Alice says. 'I understand. I think anyone would. You need relief from pain. Anger's good. Anger works. Be angry. He won't know. You're not hurting him.'

I'm not so sure. I wonder sometimes if he's lying there thinking, 'Lainey, don't. I can't help it.'

Alice puts her arm across my shoulders and squeezes a little. I have a vision, suddenly, of the two of us, as though my eyes have left my body to look down on earthbound figures casting moon shadows and sitting in their nightgowns on the wooden front steps of a house that has seen hundreds of lives come and go and still offers no comment. It's one of those eerie times of seeing myself from both the inside and out; a breathless moment, like catching a floater on your eye the right way, so that it holds still, and you can look at it. Your eye looks at your eye from behind itself and you wonder what it is you're seeing.

The bushes rustle and Maggie comes out, shakes herself off, then comes up to Alice and noses at her elbow. Alice raises her arm slightly and Maggie crawls onto her lap, settles down to grieve with us, her chin on her paws. Alice scratches behind her ears, looks at me and shrugs. 'What can I say?' She smiles. 'She's a woman dog.'

I scratch Maggie under her chin. She closes her

eyes halfway, raises her chin higher. 'Doesn't she look like Queen Elizabeth when she does that?' Alice asks.

'How come you couldn't sleep?' I ask. 'What were you thinking about?'

She stops smiling, sighs. 'You really want to know?'

'Sure.'

'I haven't told you 'cause . . . Well, you know. You've been busy. But I think Ed's . . . involved.'

'Oh, Alice. Really?'

She shrugs.

'How do you know?'

'Oh, you know. Believe me. You know.'

'What are you going to do?'

'Nothing.'

I wait.

'It'll go away. It's happened before.'

'Wow,' I say stupidly. And then, 'I had no idea.'

'Well. When you look like me . . .'

'No.'

'What do you mean, "no"?'

'I guess I mean that's a stupid reason, if that's the reason. And it's not okay, Alice.'

'You don't need to get angry on my account, Lainey.'

I'm confused, a little hurt.

'It's an accommodation I make. It's just that when a new one starts . . . Listen. He loves me. I know that. But sometimes a pretty face comes along and he can't help himself. There are such things as open marriages, you know. We have an

120

open marriage. Only we don't talk about it.'

'So do you—?'

'No. I don't.' She drains her mug, hands it back to me. 'Come on, Lainey. I know what the deal is. I'm grateful to have what I do.'

'Alice, this doesn't fit. I just don't see you putting up with this.'

'You should lower your voice. You'll wake everybody up.'

I look back at the house, then whisper, 'I don't want this to be true, Alice. I think you deserve better than this.'

She smiles. 'Well.'

'I do!'

'Lainey. The world is very different from the way you wish it were. The way you seem to pretend it is.'

I suppose it is. Once I cut an article from the newspaper and kept it on the refrigerator for almost a year. Jay asked me why I saved it and I told him it was because the article was about an ice-cream truck man, a forty-seven-year-old guy who drove around neighborhoods in the summer, playing pied-piper songs from his truck and selling ice cream to children who came running up to him in their pajamas; and that's all it was about. There was no violent, surprise ending. That's all it was about. I liked thinking about that man, taking a slow turn onto a wide neighborhood street. I made the sky a faint purple color, dusk. I gave the driver a nicely trimmed mustache, a T-shirt that smelled like detergent. I gave the children limp dollar bills that folded over in their hands. I had them line up crooked, so that each could see what the other got. I had parents watching from the doorways, the light behind them a deep yellow.

I swallow, hunch over into myself, embarrassed by my usual inability to be with the program.

'Guess what I saw today?' Alice says.

'What?' I ask miserably.

'I was at a stoplight and this guy pulls up to me, his radio's playing really loud, and he's seat-dancing, you know, and singing along.'

I straighten up. 'I love that. I love when you see people doing that.'

'Oh, but this was even better than usual. The guy pulls down the rearview mirror and checks out his hair, spits on his fingers a little to get the sides pushed back right. And then he starts wiping off his teeth with his forearm!'

'Really?'

'Yeah, he did! He was brushing his teeth with his arm!'

'Huh! Hot date, maybe.'

'Yeah, I guess.' She holds her own arm up, rubs it across her teeth. 'It tastes salty,' she says. 'Hairy. I think I'll stick with Pepsodent.'

'Right. Stick with Pepsodent,' I say. I want to add that there are some things she should not stick with, however.

When we finish our tea, I go into the house and head upstairs. I climb into bed, think about how you never quite know what really goes on in someone else's house, even when you share a common wall. Which of course we all do. I wonder if Alice has wanted to tell me this before, if she has sat alone in her living room, head in her hands, hurting, while I vacuumed or raided the refrigerator to take a bite of the Milky Way I keep hidden in the baking-soda box. I think about Ed with another woman while Alice is at home leafing through cookbooks, looking for something interesting to make for dinner. She stays home to raise Timothy, to make salad dressing from scratch; Ed whispers into the ear of another woman, who giggles and then says through her pouty, glossed lips, 'Oh, we're *bad*, aren't we?' Life is so unfair, I'm thinking. And then I laugh. As if I didn't know that.

I know I have a hard time dealing with real life. I know I glorify the past. Alice calls me Nostalgia Woman. I say, What about you, you're not so modern, you don't even work. She says that has nothing to do with it; she doesn't wish she lived fifty years ago. Well, I can't help it. Open marriage. Isn't that liberating, one person being given permission to break the other's heart. I think it was better when promises were kept. When people meant what they said, or at least tried to. I'll take the guys in bow ties working in the gas stations over sullen men slumped in chairs behind bullet-proof glass, who take your money with a kind of hatred.

The next day, when the kids are in school, I go to the grocery store with Alice. I need everything, so we go to the huge Super Save, which has what seems to be a drugstore built into the middle of it. I throw Q-Tips into my cart, then wait for Alice, who is standing in front of the boxes of hair dye. She picks one up, puts it down, picks up another, puts that down. 'What are you doing?' I ask.

'Just looking.'

'Are you going to dye your hair?'

'I might.'

'What for?'

She shrugs. 'I don't know.'

I want to ask her if she's out of her mind. I want to tell her that instead of dyeing her hair she should ask *him* to change. Instead, I pick up the ash blond, hold it up to the side of her head. 'How about this one?'

'No, not blond,' Alice says. 'I'm sure *she's* blond.'

'Right. You're probably right.'

Alice looks at my hair. 'No offense.'

'None taken. Mine's dirty blond, anyway.'

Alice picks up a box with an auburn-haired model on the front. 'You think?'

I look at the model. She is wearing a blue scarf around her perfect neck, smiling with her perfect mouth open to reveal perfect teeth. She would look quite lovely bald. 'Yeah,' I say. 'That's the one.'

Alice puts the dye in her cart next to the Cheerios, walks away too nonchalantly. Later, when I've gone to see Jay, I bet I know exactly what she'll do. She'll buy gorgeous underwear, a new nightgown not made for cold nights. I look at Alice's straight back moving away from me, sigh quietly. It happens to the best of us.

In front of the chicken bin, I tell Alice about a friend of mine who dyed her hair a different color every week. 'It was fun,' I say. 'I always kind of admired her, playing around like that.' I throw a package of drumsticks in my cart. 'That girl is the same one who used her vagina to perfume herself.' An older woman standing next to us looks up, moves away.

'She used *what*?' Alice says.

'Didn't I tell you about her? She stuck her fingers in her vagina and then rubbed the stuff behind her ears. She said it made the men crazy.'

'*That* is so dis*gust*ing,' Alice says.

'I know.'

'God!'

'I *know*.'

'Did you try it?' she asks.

'Of course.'

'Did it work?'

'Not for me.'

Alice looks over both of our carts. 'Are you done?'

'Done enough.' I hardly ever finish at the grocery store anymore.

When I get home that night, Alice comes over with a bag from Victoria's Secret. 'Nice,' I say. Over and over again. 'Nice.'

Saturday afternoon, Alice and Timothy come to the playground with us. Timothy swings listlessly, his forehead wrinkled, deeply engrossed in thought. Amy swings beside him, seeing, with each forward thrust, how far she can lean back. The idea is that her ponytail will make a design in the dirt. Sarah, who has declared herself too old for playgrounds – and is – pouts on the bench farthest away from us. She has brought a book, but she is ignoring it for the time being, focusing instead on communicating her silent anger.

'She's getting so moody,' I tell Alice. 'She's too young for PMS isn't she?'

'Who knows? Probably not.'

'No, it's not that. It's something else. I feel like she's begun this pull away from me. I know she has to do it, but it seems too soon. I'm worried that Jay's accident is making for all this unexpected fallout.'

'She's just pissed, Lainey. Let her be pissed. Of course there's fallout. This didn't just happen to Jay. It happened to all of you.'

'Yeah. I guess you're right.' I look up into the cloudless blue sky, wrestle with an impulse to stand up and scream. If I did it, the sound would reach far. Coast to coast.

'Maybe I'll come along and see Jay today,' Alice says. 'I haven't visited him since he moved.'

'That would be good. I'm trying to . . . kind of . . . approximate his normal life. It would be good for him to hear your voice.'

'What do you mean, "approximate" his life?'

'Well, just . . . you know, to put as much around him that's as familiar as possible. Smells. Fabrics. Sounds. I just thought . . . I don't know. Never mind.'

'No, I think it's a good idea,' Alice says. 'It is.' She crosses her arms, leans back against the bench, squints at our kids on the swing set. 'Timothy?' she calls, and when he looks over at her, she says, 'Why don't you play?'

'What?' he yells.

'Go run around,' Alice says. 'Go down the slide or something.'

'I'm *do*ing something,' he says.

Alice watches him for a while, then looks away. 'I don't know why I bother him. He's fine. I don't know why I think he needs to run around.' She looks back at him. 'But he does need to run around! He thinks too much. He needs to kick some rocks. He needs to beg me to play football.'

'He's only seven, Alice.'

'Yes, but he's too serious.'

'Maybe he'll be the next Einstein. Let him be. If I have to leave Sarah alone, you have to leave Timothy alone.'

'I can't. I'm his mother. I have to drive him crazy. Somebody's got to give him material for his therapist later on. I don't want him to feel deprived.'

From under the bench, Maggie rushes out to bark at a new arrival. Twin girls, one on each side of a harried-looking father. He is of the new breed, fathers trying to take equal responsibility and do the right thing, while in a secret corner of their hearts they wonder if their fathers didn't get a better deal. The twins are perhaps two, cautious-stepped and wide-eyed at the sight of a playground that is the equivalent of Disneyland for them. They choose the sandbox, begin digging distractedly.

Alice grabs Maggie, who is growling now, and pulls her up onto her lap. 'Quiet!' she says. 'You're so bad. Someone who looks like you ought to at least have a decent personality.' Something about this notion sticks in my brain. 'Wait a minute,' I want to say to Alice. 'Maggie doesn't owe anything to anybody because of the way she looks. You do know that, right?' But I don't say anything. Alice's looks are like a body of water only she knows about and we walk along the edge. Someday we'll get wet together, and she'll show me the depth of that place. But not yet.

Maggie turns around to lick Alice's face. 'Ugh,'

Alice says. 'Your breath!' Maggie licks her again, more enthusiastically. 'We should bring her to see Jay,' Alice says. 'That smell ought to get to him.'

'We should,' I say, smiling, and then, 'We should! Jay loves her! We should put her on his bed a little bit, let him feel her fur.'

'We can't bring a dog into a nursing home.'

'Why not? They have those programs where they bring puppies and kittens into nursing homes. It's good for people. It makes them happy. It lowers their blood pressure.'

Alice puts Maggie back down, holds her finger up to tell her to stay. 'Yeah, but those are planned. You can't just walk in with pets. People might be allergic.'

'We can hide her in a basket, like Toto. Jay's got a private room, nobody will see.'

'What if she barks?'

'She won't.'

'How do you know? She probably will.'

'Well, that would be good, for him to hear a dog bark. It's been a long time. It would be good.'

'Oh, all right, we'll bring her,' Alice says, and then, looking at Timothy, sighs. He has abandoned all efforts at swinging. He sits motionless, staring into space, oblivious to Amy who is squatting in the dirt beside her ponytail art, saying, 'Look, Timothy, what my hair did. Look at this! Timothy!' Her voice is a high, sweet sound, carried on spring air. I hope she keeps trying to get through to him. I hope she doesn't give up.

*　　　*　　　*

Alice follows me into the nursing home, Maggie wrapped in a tablecloth in a picnic basket. The kids stay close by. They've been instructed to make noise if Maggie starts to bark, and they are taking their job seriously, even Sarah, who is walking straight ahead but keeping her eyes sideways, on the basket. Maggie is quiet until we get to Jay's room. Then, as soon as we open the lid to take her out, she starts barking. Amid the 'Shhhhh!'s, we fail to hear the door open behind us. Then there is Gloria's voice saying, 'Y'all brought a *dog* in here?'

I turn around quickly. 'Oh. Hello, Gloria. Yes. Yes, we did. Please don't—'

'*I* don't care,' she says. 'But you'd best not let Patty see.'

'Is she working today?'

'Sure is. Bad mood, too.'

'Well . . . can you let me know if she comes?'

'I ain't got eyes in the back of my head. And I got work to do.'

We stand staring at her, all of us, until, sighing, she turns the television on. Loudly. 'There,' she says. 'That's the best I can do. But try to keep that thing quiet. What is it, anyway? Don't look like no dog I ever seen.'

'She's a very rare breed,' I say. 'First of her kind.' The kids have moved to Jay's bedside, and are trying to get Maggie to lie down beside him. She is more interested in walking around, sniffing. The bed rail holds particular allure.

'It's okay,' Alice tells them. 'Let her be. She'll

settle down in a minute.' Then, to Gloria, with her hand extended, 'I'm Alice.'

'Nice to meet you. You a friend or a relative?'

'A friend. A very good one.'

Gloria gestures with her head to the night table. 'You see what I brung him?'

In a white plastic cup, there is a piece of geranium, a bright red blossom opening on top. 'That's from a plant been in our family for years. It's the good-luck geranium, no fooling, it's brung good luck to everybody who's gotten it.'

I walk over, pick up the cup, then turn around to thank her. This is such a good thing for her to do. Last time I visited, Gloria didn't hear me come in, and she was talking to Jay, telling him about her son Lamont, the basketball player. She was embarrassed when she saw me. I wanted to say, yes, that's it, just talk to him, but I was afraid if I said it she'd never do it again. We stood looking at each other for a moment, exchanging something, and then she continued with his range of motion. 'You should be doing this for him too,' she told me gruffly and I said yes I knew that, that I did it regularly.

Now she says about the geranium, 'You plant that, when it gets its roots. And when it's big enough, you give a piece to someone else.'

'I will.'

'Okay.' She goes to the door. 'He's all washed. I just turned him and rubbed him down. Don't be putting him back over. Leave him on his side.'

'Yes, all right.'

'I'm going to close the door. If Patty comes, I didn't see a thing.'

'Right.'

'Gloria?' Amy asks. 'Is Flozell here today?'

What is it, I wonder, her fascination with him? I suppose he's the most interesting thing around here. Diversion.

'He's here every day. Drive you crazy. He's not mine, Wanda got him today.'

'Oh.'

She narrows her eyes at Amy, leans forward. 'You like him, huh?'

Amy smiles, shrugs.

'You think he's funny, right?'

'Yeah.'

'Well, I tell you what. You take care of him, how's that? Go in there and wash him up, make his bed.'

'No thank you.'

'Yeah, that's right. You right.'

Maggie settles down into the small of Jay's back, stretches out along the pillow that supports him, closes her eyes.

'Snore, Maggie,' Alice says. 'Remind him.'

Timothy scratches the top of Maggie's head. 'First she has to go to sleep,' he says. 'This ought to do it.'

Maggie's eyes close, then reopen.

'Well,' he says. 'Wait a minute.' He resumes scratching, the rest of us watching as though Timothy were dressed in God white, tools for miracles sticking out of his pockets.

Just before it's time to go, I take Amy and Sarah to the break room, give them each a handful of quarters. 'Get whatever you want,' I tell them. 'I'll come get you in just a few minutes.' They deserve a treat. They've stayed here with me long after Timothy and Alice left, without complaint.

Back in Jay's room, I lower the rail and sit beside him on the bed. 'I couldn't believe how pissed Patty got, could you? Big deal, a dog.' He breathes in, breathes out. 'Remember when we tried to free the dogs from the pound, you and me and Paul and Annie? We almost got arrested, all of us. You had a ponytail then. You looked good in a ponytail. Maybe when you come home you should grow another one. They're back in style. Everybody will think you make movies.' I sit for a while, swing my leg. 'Dolly called me the other day, from work? She's dating someone! I can't believe she's giving up on Frank. Well, not giving up. I mean, you know . . .' I hear Flozell yelling, stop talking to listen. 'Don't you *call* me by my first name!' he is saying. 'You don't even know me. Until you know me, you call me Mr Smith!'

'It's Flozell,' I tell Jay. 'He yells a lot, doesn't he? Do you hear him all the time?'

'Okay,' I say. 'I'd better go. I'll come tomorrow around noon. I'll bring your navy blue T-shirt. It's warm in here lately. You don't need long sleeves. You know, that blue one you wear all the time in the summer.'

I turn to go, and am almost out the door when I

hear something. I believe it is my name. I stand still, then walk on stiff legs back to the bedside. 'Jay? Did you call me?'

Nothing.

'Jay?'

I wait a long time, then go to get the kids.

Lainey?

As we are on our way out the door, Flozell wheels up to us. 'Well, well, well,' he says. 'It's Shirley and Hannah. And their lovely mother, Peaches.'

Sarah pointedly ignores him; Amy smiles shyly, moves in closer to me.

'Hello, Flozell,' I say.

'You bring me something today?'

'No, I didn't.'

'I got something for you.'

'Is that right?'

'That's right. I got some peach pie make you jump for joy. Johnny brought it. I'll give you a taste. She puts cream cheese on the bottom.'

'No, thank you. That's nice of you. But we're on our way out.'

'How's your husband?'

I smile, nod.

He looks at Amy. 'You come to see your daddy?'

I am getting very nervous. I look at my watch, take Amy's hand.

'I seen lots of guys like him walk right on out of here,' Flozell says. 'You got to be patient.'

'We have to go,' I say, and head out the door. I

don't know what to think about what he said. Neither do the girls. All the way back, nobody says a word, and when we get home we all go quietly to our rooms, close the doors without a sound. We remind me of nuns, minus the consolation of unswerving belief. Because despite my attempt at constant assurances to myself and others, I am well aware of the fact that there's a door number three. And I am aware of what's behind it. And what is not.

Eight o'clock in the morning. I've just gotten up, made coffee, and am now sitting staring, bleary-eyed, at the Sunday paper. I won't read a word of it. I don't know why I don't just cancel it. And yet it is comforting to come out in the morning and see two papers lying there, waiting. I put Alice and Ed's by their door, just as they do for me if they get up first. I haven't see Ed since Alice told me. I don't know how I'll behave. Things will not be the same. How can they be? It will be like he's been painted orange, and I'm not supposed to notice. If he smiles at me, it will piss me off. If he says he's going to the grocery store, do I need anything, I'll think, *Oh, yeah? The grocery store, huh? Yeah, I'll bet.*

I hear a soft knock on the door, and Alice appears in her robe. It's a faded blue quilted thing, about four hundred years old, rhinestone buttons, and she wears it with high-heeled slippers with pom-poms, given to her as a joke, but which she wears anyway. She thinks they're fun, and they don't make her feet hot as other slippers do. Among the things I like best about a good friendship are these kinds of revelations, these unveilings of selves we would never show to the world at large, though perhaps we should. Perhaps business meetings should start with people saying what they wore to bed last night. Jay used to go out for the paper in his T-shirt and boxer shorts. I always liked that, that selective boldness. He would never raise his hand in a crowd to ask a question, but he would go outside in his underwear. 'What if someone comes by and sees you?' I asked him once. And he said, after thinking for a minute, 'You know, it's never happened. But I guess I'd wave.'

Alice goes over to the coffeemaker and pours two cups, sets one down in front of me. Here is another thing I like about a good friendship, the go-aheadness of it all. You don't have to knock to come in the door. You don't have to ask to look in a refrigerator. You want coffee? Pour some. These friendships, formed by time, are getting so rare. I worry about that.

'How are you?' Alice asks, after we both take a sip of coffee.

'I don't know. Discouraged. Tired.'

'I'll bet.'

'I thought he said my name the other day.'

'You're kidding!'

'No. I was on my way out when I thought I

138

heard it. And I went over to him, but nothing happened. I waited, seemed like an hour, but nothing happened.'

Alice looks down into her cup, then up at me. 'Listen, I'm taking Timothy out to the farm today. You want to come? Why don't you come?'

Alice had a grandfather she adored who lived about thirty miles out of town on a farm. Most of the land was sold off after he died, but the family kept the house and they share it, use it for weekend retreats, hold family reunions there. I've never been there, but she and Ed go at least once a month.

'I don't think so,' I say.

'Ed's not coming.'

I look at her.

'No big deal, he just needs to get caught up on work.'

'Oh.'

'It's not what you think,' she says, a little impatiently.

'How do you know what I think?'

'Please.' She drains her cup. 'Come on, come with me. You can go see Jay, then come with me. We'll be back in time for you to visit him tonight again. You need to get out of here.'

'I don't know. I don't think I want to be so far away. There's not even a phone out there, is there?'

'No.'

'Well, I don't think so, then, Alice.'

'Lainey. What are the chances that something will happen?'

139

I get up, move to the bread drawer. 'You want toast?'

She shakes her head no. I don't either, but I slide two pieces into the toaster oven.

'Come on,' she says. 'You'd be gone maybe five hours. It would be good for you and the kids. It's like paradise there. There's a brook. A tire swing. The people next door have horses, and a fat white pony who'll stand and eat grass out of your hands all day. Come with me. It's so peaceful, Lainey.'

I watch the toast browning. Who invented this appliance? It's wonderful, really, although I once had a friend from the South and she made her toast in the oven and that tasted better. Of course, she also melted butter in a frying pan, lathered it on the toast with a basting brush. That's probably why it was so good.

'Lainey?' Alice says.

'Yeah, all right,' I say. 'After I see Jay.' I turn off the toaster. I'll give the bread to the birds later. I like watching them eat, their weighty little hops, their heads cocked left, then right, then left again. I've been doing this lately, making things and then not eating them. The other day I made a cheese sandwich, put lettuce and tomatoes on it, mayonnaise, put it on a plate, cut it in half, then threw it in the garbage.

'Are the kids coming this morning?'

'No. I'll bring them tonight. Twice a day is too much for them.' Last time we went, the kids got tired of being with Jay and asked to go to the day room. When I came to pick them up, they were

140

together on a sofa watching an old, tremulous woman sitting beside them in her nightgown and attempting to nurse a rag doll. Close by, a glassy-eyed woman sat in a wheelchair while her husband stood behind her, brushing her thin white hair. 'Yes, darling, it's all right,' he was saying. His glasses had gotten too big for his face, and he had to push them up over and over again. When I softly called the kids and they came running to me, he looked over at us and what I saw in his face was bewilderment. That's probably what he saw in mine, too.

'Go,' Alice says. 'I'll stay here till the girls wake up. I'll read the paper. They won't sleep much longer.'

True. Amy's probably up already, lying in bed doing something. She likes to play for a while in her bed before she gets up. Dress her paper dolls; string some beads; look at a book, yawning. Once she made Play-Doh pancakes, stacked them on one of her little china plates from her tea set, then brought them downstairs into the kitchen as a model for what she wanted for breakfast.

I'm like that. I like to do things in bed. I fold the laundry on the bed. Food tastes better to me when I'm under the covers. Bed is the only place to read, the best place to talk on the phone. Jay hates being in bed unless he's asleep. Or . . . you know. He would lift my hair, kiss the back of my neck, breathe out my name. I would feel the warm air travel down my back and it would chill me. That's how we almost always started. I see these videos advertised, ways to change your old routine. I never wanted to. What could be better than feeling that chill, then turning around into arms you'd memorized years ago?

I head for the stairs. Alice turns to the front page. She'll read whole articles. It always seems like such a hard job to me to have to dig for the rest of the story on another page. I'll read the front page sometimes, but then I'll not bother to finish the story if I have to turn to another page. It's not always laziness. Oftentimes, it's fear. Oftentimes, in fact, I don't even get through the part on the front page. I get astounded. I get sad. I turn to the recipes for relief. Once, when I found something good I wanted to make and started to write down what I'd need to buy at the store I saw that my hand was shaking. And this was long before Jay got hurt. Small wonder, now that disaster has moved off the newspaper page and into my kitchen, that I have had to create Evie to tell me soothing stories. Domestic lullabies. Really, I should cancel the paper.

Wanda has Jay today. She is filling up the basin for a bed bath when I come in the room. I hold out my hand, introduce myself.

'Yes, I know your name,' she says. 'We talk about you sometimes.' Then, hastily, 'Nicely.'

I wonder what that means.

'I can bathe him if you're busy,' I tell her.

She puts the basin on the bedside stand, pours some oil in it. 'That's okay. We have a lot of help today. I've only got five others. They're done already.'

I look at my watch. Nine-thirty.

Wanda lowers the head of Jay's bed, begins to wash his face. She is tender, thorough. She makes a little mitt of the washcloth so water doesn't drip off the ends. You don't always see that. Most times Jay's face gets scrubbed like a kitchen floor. But Wanda is the kind of nurse who takes her training seriously, the kind who won't hold dirty linen against her uniform, the kind you see washing her hands in the little sink out in the hall many times a day. I sit down in the chair, watch her. She's a very pretty girl, honey-blond hair pulled back into a braid, clear blue eyes, cheeks a nice pink color without the assistance of makeup. She wears tiny gold hoops in her ears. Her uniforms have flowers embroidered here and there – you have to look closely, because it's white on white. I wonder if she does it herself.

'You're new, huh?' I say.

'I've been here about three weeks now. I used to work at St Mary's. In the oncology unit.'

'You didn't like that?'

She turns around. 'Oh, no. I loved it. They had a problem with my . . . Well, the truth is I got fired.'

I stifle an impulse to leap up and grab the washcloth away from her. Instead, I begin watching her more carefully.

'I'll tell you about it,' she says. 'It wasn't for incompetence or anything. But for now, just let me . . . I'd like to just pay attention to him.'

'Of course.'

She turns back to Jay, starts talking to him in a low, friendly voice. Her new car, she's talking about. Five speed. Moves out. Smells like leather, though there's none in the car. Paid sticker price, couldn't help it. And then how her garden has been planned, what vegetables she and her husband will harvest in the summer. 'You'll be out of here by then, of course,' she tells him. 'I'll bring some tomatoes over to your house; you can make

144

your kids some BLT₃. Your daughters are beautiful, Jay.' I lean back in my chair, and one-twentieth of my brain says wearily, 'Say thank you, Jay.'

When she gets to his hand, Wanda exercises each finger independently, then moves all of them together. Yes, that's right. She's doing it right. I'll go get a cup of coffee.

In the day room, I see Flozell sitting by the window with Johnny. And then see that a baby is lying in his lap. I stop, stare, then go up to him. When he sees me coming, he pulls the blanket down from a tiny, sleeping face. The baby is beautiful, curly eyelashes, a dimpled chin, hands resting across a chest not much bigger than a silver dollar. 'Who's this?' I whisper.

'My daughter!' he says. Not in a whisper. The baby startles, then stills. 'Premature, but she out the hospital now. She fine.'

'What's her name?' I ask.

'Tanesha,' Johnny says, at the same time that Flozell says, 'Name is Jacqueline, after you know who.'

'My ass,' Johnny says, with what I can only describe as a kind of misplaced elegance. She speaks quietly, down her nose, as though she is saying, 'Indeed.' She is quite beautiful, really; and so petite, she can't be over 5' 1". I wonder how she created this baby with Flozell. Surely he didn't lie on top of her. He'd kill her. She is dressed in a floral print polyester dress, ruffles along the bottom and the top. A black leather jacket rests on her lap. Beside her, a huge black purse gapes open,

145

revealing a pack of cigarettes, a gold cosmetics bag, a key ring with a rose captured in a plastic heart. 'I'm the one had this baby and I'm the one named her. It's on her birth certificate. I called her "Tanesha." Ain't nothing he can do about it.'

''Cept call her Jacqueline,' he says. 'That's just what I intend to do, call her Jac-que-line.'

Johnny chews her gum for a while, swinging her crossed leg and watching him with slit-eyed affection. Then, 'You call her that, she stare right into space. She ignore you. You ain't around enough to have no influence on her.'

Flozell looks down at the sleeping face. His lower lip is pushed out. He is pouting magnificently.

'How's your husband?' Johnny asks me.

'He's being bathed,' I say, as though that answers the question. Johnny nods, looks down at her purse, sad for me. The first time I met her, she asked, 'What's wrong wid your man?' She was wearing large hoop earrings and I remember staring at one of them when I told her. She blinked, then said, 'Whew, Lord!' She reached out for my arm, squeezed it.

'I just came in here for coffee,' I tell her. 'Can I get you some?'

'No thanks,' she says, and then, to Flozell, 'Give me that baby back now.'

'Not yet,' he says. 'No.'

'Sheeeit.' Johnny resettles herself in her chair, smiling so widely I can see the gold repair on one of her back molars.

146

I fill a plastic cup half full of the day room's awful coffee, carry it back to Jay's room. Wanda is pulling his covers over him. 'All done,' she says. The odor of ironed sheets is in the air. Everything in his room has been straightened, cleaned. The bottles on top of his nightstand are lined up, the telephone dusted.

I walk over, kiss his cheek, put my hand on the top of his head, look closely into his face. 'Jay,' I say. 'I'm here.'

I wait a moment, then straighten, look over at Wanda. She is standing by the door, watching me.

'So what do *you* think?' I say.

'I think all things are possible,' she says. 'I think what we don't know about medicine is as vast as outer space. Is that what you meant?'

'Yes. Thank you.'

She opens the door. 'I'll be right back. I need to hang his feeding.'

I sit on the bed, take Jay's hand. 'Breakfast time, Jay. What do you want?'

As if I didn't know. Regular coffee in his regular cup at his regular table. He has a cup that has a Corvette on it. The picture of the white '56 has nearly faded away. We went to look at Corvettes once. Jay sat behind the wheel, and I watched him from the front of the car. It was a new one. I told him I didn't like it, that it looked like a Dustbuster, but I did like it, mostly for the way Jay's face looked when he turned on the headlights and they came flipping up out of the body of the car. I thought, when those kids are done with college, we're taking out a loan and buying one of these. Even if we have bifocals.

'I just saw Flozell's baby,' I tell Jay. 'He has a baby! And she's so beautiful. You remember when Sarah was born and the doctor told you to tell me what sex she was? And you weren't quite sure, because the umbilical cord confused you?' I smile down at him. If I try, I can imagine that his eyes are only closed to hear me better. 'We were supposed to have a fancy dinner, but it was too late at night,' I say. 'So they brought us all the stuff they could find from the little kitchen there, remember? We got toast and jelly . . . Jell-O, graham crackers . . . what else? I don't know, it didn't matter, everything tasted wonderful. And I remember you had some apple juice and you started to toast Sarah, you held this little flowered paper cup up to her and started to say something and then you just started crying and then I started crying. Everybody cries about babies, huh, Jay? Maybe we should have another one.' I say things like that sometimes, and then immediately feel as though some bottom has dropped out, as though I'm driving along and the road suddenly disappears. And I am sitting there, suspended in black space, my hands fiercely clenching the steering wheel as though I still had some control. I shouldn't say things like that.

Wanda comes in carrying Jay's feeding and I get out of the way, go to sit in the corner. After the stuff starts dripping in, she pulls an extra chair up

148

to sit beside me. 'I'd like to tell you what happened, why I got fired.'

'You don't have to.'

'I want to.'

'All right.' Actually, I do want to know.

'I was working nights,' she says. 'There was a woman who was dying, Irene was her name, sweet woman, and she had these sandals she kept at the side of the bed. They were so small. She never used them, she was too weak to get up, she just wanted them there. I think she thought maybe if she kept them there, she'd get to use them again. And I also think it was a way for us to know her – you know, a way of her saying, "Look, I wasn't always a patient lying here in this bed. I went shopping. These are the shoes I picked out."'

She looks at me, and I nod.

'Anyway,' Wanda says, 'she was in a lot of pain. I'd been taking care of her for a long time, a few weeks; every time I was on, I had her. I knew this was going to be the night that she died. After a while, you can just tell.

'It was really busy when you worked nights, you had at least eleven patients, you didn't ever have time to sit with any of them. I went in to see her as often as I could, I increased her morphine drip, I turned her and rubbed her back, but it wasn't enough. She was really restless. She asked me to put her on the floor. I said I couldn't do that. She said, Why not, she wanted to be on the floor, she was so sick of the bed, it was making her feel crazy to be in that bed. She wanted to be on the floor where there was more room. So I said, Fine, and I put a bunch of blankets down and got an aide to help me and we put her on the floor. And she smiled at me and said thank you. And the next time I came in she had died. I called the resident to pronounce her, and he said, What the hell was she doing on the floor? And I told him. He told someone else, and the next time I came to work they told me to punch out, I was fired.'

She smiles ruefully at me, shrugs. 'And that was it. They were not interested in any explanations. They didn't care that the other nurses all tried to defend me. They didn't care that all my evaluations had been excellent.'

I don't know what to think about what she has told me. I don't think what she did was wrong, yet it doesn't seem quite right, either. Suppose Jay woke up and asked her to put him on the floor. Suppose I walked in and found him there, wouldn't I be angry? But he would say, 'No, Lainey, I asked for this.' Unless he was dead. Suppose I came in and he was dead on the floor. Wouldn't I be angry? Even if I knew he'd asked to be put there? I don't know. I don't know. I don't want to think about it.

'What made you become a nurse?' I ask Wanda.

'Oh well, I wanted . . . I had a need to express my compassion. I wanted to help.' She looks carefully at my face. 'I care for people. They don't always let you show that.'

'No.'

She leans back, sighs. 'I'll tell you, nursing

school was murder. Once we were learning about hearts, and the instructor held up a beef heart – that's what we had to study, a heart from a cow, only the medical students got to look at a human heart. But anyway, he stuck his finger through a valve to show us the connection between the atrium and the ventricle, then wiggled it a little like he was playing a game, and I passed out. Not because it was gross. Because it was unholy. I understood we needed to learn. But I thought we should learn with reverence. I mean, there was a cow, born to a mother cow, living on the earth, and now here was that cow's heart in the hand of a human who was making fun of it.'

'Yes,' I say, as though I know exactly what she is talking about. And I sort of do.

'From the time I first started nursing,' she says, 'patients would do things for me they wouldn't do for other nurses.'

'Like what?'

'Well, once I took care of this woman psychiatrist who'd been horrible to all the other nurses, she was really hard to get along with. She wouldn't let anyone bathe her, and she was bedridden, believe me, she needed to get bathed. By the end of the day, I'd washed her. Turned out she was embarrassed to have anyone see her feet. Isn't that amazing? I mean, the tenderness of that?'

I smile.

'And then when I was just an aide, a woman who'd had a colostomy picked me to be the one to ask about sex. She told me to close the door and then she said, "What about my husband? How does one have sex with this thing?" She was quite formal, you know, a very rich woman, lying in bed in her turquoise negligee, her face all made up. "How does *one* have sex?" I was sort of scared, but I knew she needed me to tell her something. I knew she wouldn't ask anyone else. So I said, "Well, you just take off the bag and tape a little cotton square over the stoma. And then you forget about it. Because that's not what he's making love to." And then I asked her what was so attractive about the original exit, anyway. You know. A stoma is no worse than an asshole, was my opinion.'

She leans forward again, speaks softly. 'I'm just trying to tell you I know what you're doing with all these things around your husband — his clothes, the kids' drawings, all the things you bring in from home. And the way you talk to him, read to him. I support you one hundred percent. I think it really helps.'

I look back at her, and my heart feels like a full bucket, hanging heavy in my chest. 'Do you really?'

'Yes.'

'The kids have started doing it too,' I tell her. 'They tell him little stories. Well, the younger one, Amy, does. Sarah's still not sure. But she's starting to come around. Last time we visited she told him she'd gotten an *A* on a test just before we left. She sort of yelled it from the middle of the room. I hope it's okay. I hope it's not . . . I don't know, damaging or anything for them.'

'I think it's fine. I think it's a good way for them to feel like they're doing something too. And may I tell you something? I also think you should take care of yourself. You can crack up a little when these things go on for so long. You've got to bring a healthy self in here. That will help him most. He needs to feel your strength. And you need to do what you have to to keep it.'

'Well, yes, I know. I know that. In fact, I just wanted to see him this morning, and then I'm going away all day. To a farm, with my neighbor and our children. To relax.'

'Good.'

I pick up my purse, pull it tight against my belly. 'So, do you . . . honestly now, do you really think there's a chance he'll come home?'

'I absolutely do.'

'Yes. Well, I believe it too. I don't know that anyone else does, though.'

'You'd be surprised. When I told you we talk about you, that's because we admire you.'

I put my hands over my face, start to cry. Wanda puts her hand on my shoulder, speaks softly. 'We're going to get him back to you, Mrs Berman.'

I nod, sniff loudly. 'Please call me "Lainey."'

'Okay. You know what the nurses where I used to work called me?'

'What?'

'"Wonder."'

'Oh. That's good.'

'Yes, I thought so, too.' She stands up. 'Go out to the country. Have a good time. And don't worry, we'll take care of him.'

I come out into the hall, close the door quietly. I'm a little nervous. I wonder if I've said too much. I feel as though I've unzipped myself and handed my shy insides to a nurse named Wonder. If that was a mistake, it's too late now.

Alice and I are sitting at the edge of the brook, making circles in the water with our winter-white feet. The water is so clear it's nearly invisible, so cold it feels like it's biting. Still, when winter is newly gone and you can sit on the grass, it's hard to pass up a stream running at your feet. We dangle past the point of ache and into numbness, then pull our feet out for a while, hold them in our hands to warm them. The kids are letting caterpillars crawl up the inside of their arms for the sticky tickle, shrieking out their pleasure. I have an image of the caterpillars rolling their eyes.

'I wish I could live here.' Alice sighs, reaching out to stroke the low-hanging leaves of the tree beside her.

'Why don't you?'

'Oh, you know. Jobs. Schools. Plus once I got here I probably wouldn't like it anymore. I'd miss having things close by: movies, the dry cleaners. Broccoli. You know.'

'Yeah. And me. You'd miss me, right?'

She smiles, dips her fingers into the brook, flips water at me. Confirmation. Then, leaning back on her elbows, she says, 'Isn't it lucky that we live next door to each other? I never liked my neighbors before. Well, I liked them, but I couldn't really be friends with them. Not like with you and Jay.'

Jay. I realize I have actually had a moment of not thinking of him. But now his spirit wedges itself between the two of us. If he were here, he'd put his feet in the water too, maybe stand up and walk down the stream a ways. And then he'd turn back, look toward me, hold out a hand. We shared. Whenever possible, that's what we did. Fudgsicles. Quilts. The pleasant burden of raising children. Money, and the lack of it. Once, when it was a week until payday and we had only a five-dollar bill left, we started fighting about what to do with it. Finally, Jay lit a burner on the stove and stuck the money in the flame, burned it right up. I couldn't believe it. I stood there crying, saying, 'Jesus, Jay, we could have gotten groceries. Why did you do that?' And he said it was because we weren't ever going to do that again, fight about money. That we would never allow it to become that important in our lives. And we haven't. It's funny; I came from a family that was very, very 'comfortable' financially, but I feel more comfortable now.

God, I miss him. I sigh, shake my head.

'I'm sorry,' Alice says, 'I shouldn't have brought him up. I knew it as soon as I said it. But it was too late, then. I hate when I do that.'

'It's all right.'

Alice looks over at the kids, then back at me. 'Let's talk about my misery, so you'll feel better. Do you think I should divorce Ed?'

It surprises me, that she would say this. I feel kind of punched. But then I think of all the times I felt so odd around Ed. The way I couldn't quite ever connect with him. I would get the feeling, when he was looking right at me and talking, that he still wasn't looking at me. That he wasn't quite present. Maybe Alice feels like that.

I remember a time Ed was out playing football with the kids. They were having a great time, and I was smiling, watching from the window, thinking, Why am I so nasty about him? He's a nice guy. He's just shy or something. He stopped playing, told the kids he needed to rest, and went to sit on the porch steps. I almost went out with him. I was thinking I'd sit down, maybe offer him a beer. I was thinking if only I'd try harder, I'd get to know him, and then I'd like him. But before I could go out with him, Alice did. She sat beside him and he moved just the slightest bit away. It was tiny – he didn't move anything but his shoulder, so that it wouldn't be resting against hers. I thought it was so awful. I thought, what is this? And I thought if I had to put a name on that kind of behavior I would say it was withholding.

And I would say that it is one of the worst kinds of poisons that exist in human relationships.

When Ed pulled away from Alice, a thin blade of sunlight pushed its way between them. I had to look away. It was hurting my eyes.

I am tempted to say to Alice, 'You know, the truth is I never liked Ed. Never trusted him. You can do much better.' But that is so dangerous. And so I only say, 'Well, I don't know if you should think about divorce already. I mean, have you even talked about it?'

'No.'

'Not any of the times that it happened?'

'No. But I . . . It didn't happen before.'

'I thought you told me it had!'

'I did say that. I thought it would make it easier to deal with, to say it had happened before. That it was just an arrangement, something I was used to. I thought maybe it wouldn't hurt so much then. But this is the first time, at least as far as I know. And it's so weird. It's so weird. One minute I want to do anything to keep him. The next I want to leave. Just leave. Or tell him to.'

'Do you know who it is? The woman?'

She shakes her head. 'No. Someone he works with, I'm sure. I can see her getting ready for work, fixing her hair, checking her teeth, thinking, *I wonder when he'll be in today. I wonder if we'll have time to do it. I wonder when he'll get rid of his dippy wife.* Whenever he sees her, she's all put together. Pretty gold earrings on clean ears, perfume behind them. Her underwear matches.

158

She's not in her bathrobe, lying around with menstrual cramps, farting.'

'I have to tell you something, Alice.'

'What?'

'You look fabulous in your bathrobe.'

She looks at me.

'I mean it.'

'Right. See, I know you mean it. I know you do. But Ed's not the kind to think like that. He likes . . . Huh. You know what? I don't know. I don't know what he likes. I mean, he's eating dinner and he says he likes the chicken and I think, *Do you really? Or is this bullshit too?* We watch a movie, and I think, *Are you really watching this? Or are you thinking about her?* I hate him, is the thing. Which is very inconvenient, because I love him.'

'Alice, you've got to talk about it.'

'I don't want to. I just don't. I've been waiting for this. Now it's happened. What's to talk about?'

Everything, it seems to me. But it's not my job to drive Alice's car. It's my job to verify the scenery.

'Well, should we feed the kids?' she asks.

'Are you hungry?'

'Sure.'

No, she isn't. But we call the kids over to us. When they sit on the blanket, I see grass stains on their knees, wild-flowers tucked behind their ears. I'm so glad we came. Alice and I will handle the trouble off to the side. Let their brains be taken up with spring.

Pat Swanson meets us when we come in the door to the nursing home that evening. 'Could I see you for just a minute?' she asks.

I tell the kids to go ahead, and follow Pat into her tiny office. She's got a yellowing philodendron in a basket on her windowsill, stacks of papers that nearly obscure a dusty photograph on her desk, a gigantic schedule taped to the wall. She points to a chair beside her desk, then sits in her own. 'So. How are you doing?'

'I'm fine. I'm surprised to see you here.'

'Oh, I work an odd shift every now and then. Check up on how things go during the off hours. I even come in and do a night sometimes.'

'Oh. That's good.' I notice that her mascara is blue. Midnight blue, I think they call it. I never understood blue mascara.

'The reason I wanted to speak to you is . . . well, I just wanted to give you a kind of progress report.

160

You must be wondering how your husband's doing.'

'I do visit him every day. I see how he's doing.'

'Uh-huh.'

'I know he's not in, you know, great shape or anything. But he's holding his own.'

'Yes. He's holding his own. I guess you could say that.'

'Right.'

'Look, I have to tell you, Mrs Berman, the doctors don't have much hope that your husband will wake up.'

I swallow. Jerks, standing in front of their too-expensive bathroom mirrors each morning, shaving their uplifted chins.

'One thing we needed to know is whether or not you wanted what we call heroic measures. That's when—'

'I know exactly what heroic measures are,' I say. 'And yes, I want them. In fact, you can station the crash cart – that's what you call it, isn't it? The crash cart? – you can station that right outside his room. You can draw up every medication in it, just in case.' *Lainey,* Jay would say quietly, when I would get going this way. He doesn't get nasty like I do. He's kinder.

Pat nods, slowly. 'All right. I guess I understand what your wishes are.'

I stand. 'I intend to bring him home. Recovered.'

Nothing. Polite vacancy.

'If you don't think that's possible, I'd like you to stay out of his room.'

'I'm the head nurse here, Mrs Berman. I go into every patient's room, every day.'

'Well, don't talk to him,' I say. 'Don't touch him.' I leave her office, walk down the hall rapidly, then slowly. I shouldn't have done that. She has too much power. I need her on my side. Later, I'll apologize. Maybe.

The kids have put flowers from the farm on Jay's windowsill. Beside the vase is a pile of stones. 'Where'd you get the rocks?' I ask.

'They were here,' Amy says.

Sarah reaches for one, brings it over to me. 'This one has a picture on it. See?'

What she hands me is a fetish stone, which I know is believed to hold a spirit. There's a bird etched into it, a long-beaked creature, his eyes directed fearlessly forward, tail feathers streaming straight out behind him. I don't know who brought it, I only know it's here. And I accept it with profound ignorance and thanks, which is what we do with all miracles.

I can feel you. Listen. I can feel you all. Come closer. It's so warm. Oh, here, the little weight of my daughter next to me, the feel of her hand on my forehead. Skin to skin, can you hear me, Amy? A pulling up, a rising in my chest, a flutter. And now I feel . . . Look. Is my finger alive, moving? I can't open my eyes, what is so heavy on them? A serpentine tunnel. This convoluted blackness.

'His eyeballs are moving,' Sarah says. 'It's gross.' She is leaning against the wall by the

162

window, her hands tucked behind her. Amy, who'd been sitting on the bed beside Jay, stroking his face, pulls her hand away.

I cross in front of Sarah, give her a severe look, sit down on the other side of Jay. I pick up one of his hands, wrap my own around it. Someone cut his nails today. 'Hi, honey,' I say. 'We're here. Just relax. We're here. We went to the country today, to Alice's farm. It was so beautiful.'

He stops his small movements, quiets. There! Don't they see things like that? Pat Swanson, hasn't she seen this? He's listening! Isn't he?

'We saw a fox,' Amy tells him.

'Did not,' Sarah says.

'Did so!'

'Girls,' I say.

'It wasn't a fox,' Sarah says. 'It was a dog.'

'No way, I saw it and it had a bushy tail. And so did Timothy, he said it was a fox, too. And he knows every animal.'

'You're crazy.'

'Sarah,' I say. 'Stop.'

'I don't care,' she says. 'I don't even want to be here.'

I stand up, take her arm and pull her out of the room. Down the hall a little ways I ask, 'What is the matter with you? Do you think he needs to hear that?' I am speaking between clenched teeth, in a low voice I barely recognize as my own. I am full of the dangerous kind of fury that comes from pain.

Sarah says nothing. The line of her mouth has

163

thinned, hardened. She is full of the same kind of fury.

'I asked you a question!' I say.

'*What?*'

'I *asked* you, do you think he needs to *hear* that?'

'Hear what?'

'Sarah, don't you do this. Do not do this. You know exactly what I'm talking about. I want you to behave in front of Dad. I don't want him to hear you two fighting.'

'He can't hear us anyway.'

'Why do you say that!'

'He never does anything back. Not one thing. He just lies there. I don't see why you think he can hear you. And I don't see why we have to come. It's creepy. And it doesn't do any good. It doesn't do anything!'

Down the hall, one of the patients wheels toward us, an old man wearing a stained white T-shirt and brown trousers. He wheels slowly, his head hanging down, his half-full urinal stuck between his knees. I take Sarah by the hand, lead her into the nearby kitchen. 'Sarah, I don't expect you to understand all this. *I* don't understand all this. But I believe it's important to talk to Dad, to let him know we love him and that we expect him to get better. I really, really believe he will get better.'

Sarah opens one of the metal drawers of the tiny cabinet, closes it.

'Can you just . . . I want you to try too, Sarah.

This is our family. We work together. We need to work together.'

She looks up into my face and her eyes fill. 'He's so skinny, now.'

'Yes. I know. He looks different.'

And now, sobbing, she says, 'I can't help it. He's so weird. He's not even like my dad.'

I hold her against me. I have such a strong longing to cry with her, but somebody has to be the mother. I take in a deep breath, talk in a calm voice to the top of her head. 'Well, he's not like he used to be. That's true. He's sick now. You know, you can look really bad when you're sick. We just need to help him get better. And then he'll come home and help take care of you when you get sick.'

She pulls away from me. 'I won't ever be sick like that!'

'No. No, you won't, Sarah.'

'Will I?'

'No! It's not contagious, it was an accident. It was ice! Remember?'

Silence. And then, 'Yes. I remember.'

'It was so rare, Sarah. An accident, what they call a freak accident. I don't believe it will ever happen again. Okay?'

She nods.

'All right. So listen. You just need to try to remember that it's Dad in there. No matter how he looks, it's Dad.'

'Okay.' She closes her eyes tightly, then opens them and looks up at me. 'I think we should put a

165

picture of him in his room. On the windowsill. Of how he used to be.'

'I think that's a terrific idea.' It is. Let everyone see him with his sweatshirt and jeans on, holding a basketball at his side, his hair sexily messy, his teeth white and strong, his watch ticking on his wrist. Let Pat Swanson see. Let the doctors who want to let him go see. And let Sarah see. Let her have something in his room to look at to remind her of why she is here. Because it's easy to forget. Even for me. Sometimes, sitting beside him and blathering on and on, I get the feeling that my real self has picked up my purse and left.

After the kids are asleep, I come down into the kitchen for a piece of chocolate cake, left over from our picnic. The light is so dim. I've got to replace that bulb. I start to think about asking Ed to help me, then remember. I'll figure it out myself. I'll ask at the hardware store.

'Coffee in the batter gives chocolate cake a very nice taste,' Evie says. ''Course, it has to be strong. And buttermilk, that's good in there, too.'

I stare at my plate, continue eating. I know where she is. Opposite me. Sitting.

'You had quite a day today. It can be very difficult with children. You never feel as much love toward anyone else. Or as much anger. Not much of a chance for you to talk about it, either. It's harder for you women today. I feel sorry for you. We had each other around. The kids were right outside, playing, going in and out of one another's houses like they lived in every one of

167

them, and we women, we were there, too. Sometimes a couple of us would be out on the sidewalk
just talking and then pretty soon, why, there'd be
a regular crowd out there. There were plenty of
times we sat on someone's front steps, giving
advice, getting it. Oh, we solved some problems,
I'll tell you! Used to wonder why the White House
didn't call us, we'd tell them what to do, all right.'

I think about whether or not I want another
piece of cake. No. Yes. I get up to get another slice,
sit down again and start eating it.

'Every night, we waited for the men to come
home,' Evie says. 'We'd take off our aprons, run a
comb through our hair, put on a little lipstick,
watch at the window. That's the way we did it, we
were told to make a man feel welcome when he
came home. We were told, "Clear away the
clutter, minimize the noise, let him relax after his
hard day. Don't tell him any problems." Well, I
never did go along with that one. My problems
were his problems. That's the way I looked at it.
And vice versa, of course. It was a partnership. I
didn't mind getting a little gussied up for dinner,
though. I think I did it for myself as much as him. I
didn't mind a little rouge and lipstick making me
look better. I liked it.

'And the men, they had their routines for
coming home, too. I believe they might have
tidied up a bit themselves. My husband, he
always tooted the horn when he pulled into the
driveway. Then the kids knew it was time to wash
up for dinner.

'It was a community, don't you see, all of us doing more or less the same thing, all of us full of a kind of hope you don't have now. The isolation you people live with, it kind of infects everyone, makes you sick. Don't you see that you need each other? I wonder sometimes, do you even know what you're after?'

I put my fork down, rest my forehead in my hand. I recall once having a dream where I was on an airplane and I stood up from my seat, turned around to look at all that was around me. The sun was coming in the windows of the plane, illuminating the passengers. Some were really old, and some were children, and everyone was asleep, bathed in this golden light. I found it so moving, seeing all these people hurtling through the air in a long silver tube, sleeping, their hands in their laps. And I heard a voice say, 'You see? They're all fetuses.' I told Jay the dream the next morning, when the sun coming through the kitchen window was bathing him, in his work suit. And he said it was a very tender dream and did I know what it meant and I said no. But I did know. I just couldn't say it in words.

Then, as though it is related, I recall something else. I once sat behind two women at a movie. They looked to be in their late forties and they were talking about how self-sufficient their children were, now that they were teenagers. 'So what do you think comes next?' one of them said. 'I mean, now that we're not needed anymore? Do we just get decrepit? Do we work even longer

169

hours just to fill the void?' The other one ate a handful of popcorn and then said, 'I don't know.'

I pick up my saucer to lick off the plate. Crumbs fall onto my lap and I brush them onto the floor.

'Better sweep those crumbs up pretty quick,' the ghost woman says. 'Ants will be here before you know it. I had good luck keeping them away with a mix of cloves and red pepper. They don't care for that. Just sprinkle it along the doorways.'

I look up, slowly, and see her, a dim, vague presence, sitting at the table in a robe with a scarf knotted around her head. She has her hair in pincurls. She sees me looking at them and says, 'Coming up, my sisters and I used rags to curl our hair. That worked better. There were six of us, and we slept three in a bed, can you imagine? We'd tell each other stories every night before we went to sleep. At first, it was ghost stories. But then, when we got older, it was on to our fellows.'

I sit immobile, aware of a spreading pain in my chest.

She speaks softly. 'You just don't know, do you? You think he might die, and what will you do if he dies? It's always a shock, I'll tell you, no matter how it happens. I remember the night Walter died. December fourteenth, about seven in the evening. He was two weeks past being sixty-eight years old. He was sitting in the armchair watching television and he had a real quiet heart attack. I came in to tell him to get washed up, dinner was almost ready, and he didn't move. I knew right away. He was just gone. It was a shell

170

sitting there. I stood across the room from him for a little while. I remember I was wiping my hands dry on my apron the whole time, just staring at him. Finally, I called the doctor, and then I tried to get him to lie down, I thought if he was dead he should be lying down. I got him onto the floor, and I was talking to him the whole time, saying "Now Walter, you're going to have to cooperate with me." Just like that. Well, you don't want to let go at first, you see. You just can't. I covered him with the afghan I'd just finished making the week before, he'd picked some of the colors. And then I sat down next to him and I just waited. I'll tell you, my nerves were jumping, but I sat so very still. I was thinking I was so glad I'd been fixing him a dinner he liked – his favorite, in fact. He liked pot roast, overdone so the meat would be sticking to the pan something awful, he liked that. I never did eat any of that dinner. I saved it in the refrigerator for close to a month, and then I threw it away. In that cupboard right there. Same place as you keep your garbage. Threw the whole pan out.'

I take in a breath, start to say something, then don't.

'The night before, we'd been to the Carnation Ballroom. I used to get my hair done once a month, cost me fifty cents to get it all poofy, and then we'd go out dancing. Yes, we'd had a good time. It helped me later, to think about that.'

'Please,' I whisper. I want so much for her to go away. And she does.

In the morning, I awaken to the sounds of kids talking. I come down to start coffee and see Sarah, Amy and Timothy sitting at the kitchen table before empty bowls. They are dressed already. I look at the clock and see why: it's ten-fifty.

'Are you sick?' Amy asks.

'No,' I say. 'Just tired, I guess.' I feel terrible that they got their own breakfast, even though they like doing that. It's their chance to eat with odd things: cereal poured in a coffee cup, then eaten with a fork; a sandwich served on the lid of a Dutch oven. They think it's fun. Once Amy poured orange juice over spoon-sized Shredded Wheat, then ate it with chopsticks.

I start the coffee, sit at the table with them. 'What are you guys up to?'

'My parents went out somewhere,' Timothy said. 'They told me to stay here. They thought you were up, you always get up early.'

'I do, usually. I'm sorry I was asleep.'

'It's okay.' His voice is so tiny, his forgiveness so vast.

But it's not okay. I need to tell Alice never to do that again, leave without telling me.

'Where did they go?' I ask Timothy.

'I don't know. They were in a bad mood.'

'How come?' Amy asks, as though she's reading my mind and asking for me.

He shrugs, pushes his glasses up on his nose. 'Beats me. Let's go finish.'

'Finish what?' I ask. 'What are you doing?'

'A play,' Timothy says.

'Really!'

'Yes.'

'Can I watch?'

'No,' Sarah says.

'Yes, she can,' Amy says, and it occurs to me to say, Come along, Amy. I'm going to take you to a toy store and you can have everything.

'It's not ready yet,' Sarah says. 'We're practicing.' She's being evasive. But she is entitled to her privacy.

'Okay,' I say.

I go to the cupboard, take down a mug, have a flash of memory about last night. Maybe I need to call a therapist. I pour milk into the creamer, sit at the table to wait for the coffee to finish. I watch the kids as they pile out the door. They are all talking at once, all hearing what each one is saying, I'm sure. The other day I found Sarah in front of the television. The stereo was on, a book was in her lap, and she was talking on the phone. 'Turn something off!' I said. And she said why? And I said because she couldn't do all those things at once, and she said sure she could. I think she was right. We get narrow in our old age. We lose so many talents.

I heard the door slam, see Amy come back in. She stands before me for a second, then says, 'You're not sick?'

'No, I'm really not, Amy.'

She goes back out, hollering, 'Wait! Don't start yet!' She is wearing shorts, which are on backwards. Over them is her pink tutu, worn once in a dance recital. At least she's getting some use out of it. And on top, a sweatshirt and a plastic necklace featuring glitter and water captured in a plastic heart. Why don't we elect little children to Congress, I wonder? Why don't we let them run things? They have such fine imaginations. They are almost always in a good mood.

I pour the small amount of coffee that has dripped into the carafe into my mug, then stand at the window, watching. Timothy lies on the ground, puts his arms across his chest and closes his eyes. Sarah and Amy stand on one side of him, then squat down and start to roll him over. 'Ow!' he says, and opens his eyes, sits up. 'You're hurting me! Don't make your fingers so pointy!'

Sarah stands up, hands on her hips. 'You're such a baby. Just shut up. Anyway, you can't talk. You're in a coma, stupid.'

I back away from the window. I don't want to

watch this. Then I go back over to it. Yes, I do.

'Close your eyes,' Amy says. 'This is the part when you're going to die.'

I take back every tender thought I ever had about children. They are little savages. I open the window wide, yell out, 'Hey!'

They all look up. 'You stop fighting or I'll make you all come in here.'

'We're not fighting,' Sarah says.

'I heard you.'

'It wasn't fighting,' Timothy says. 'They were just hurting me. Accidentally. It wasn't malicious.'

'Why don't you just come in and play?' I say. 'Why don't you come in and we'll make cookies? Chocolate chip.'

They stand still for a moment, and then Sarah says, 'Mooooom! Just close the window.'

I do. I don't want to hear this after all. They are going to face what I never can.

Amy and Timothy are watching television when Alice comes home. Sarah is at a friend's house until after dinner.

Alice greets the kids with a weary cheerfulness, then comes into the kitchen with me, slouches in a chair, her legs straight out before her. 'Well. We had quite a talk. The upshot of which is, he denies everything.' Then, looking up at me, 'I think he's scared. He wants to talk to you.'

'Oh, God, Alice, I don't want to get in the middle of this.'

175

'You're not in the middle. You're on my side.'

'I can't talk to him. I need to go see Jay.'

'Yeah, I know. Afterward. When you come back. Okay?'

I don't answer.

'Okay?'

'Well . . . I don't know, Alice. Do you really want me to?' If she really wants me to, I have to. I owe her and owe her and owe her.

'Lainey, I feel like my head is spaghetti. My brain. I'm so confused. I want you to talk to him and listen to what he says and then tell me what he means. I just don't know anymore. God! I'm in a bad mood! It's like walking around in an itchy coat. I don't feel like dealing with anything.'

'You want me to take Timothy with me to the nursing home?'

'Oh, I don't know. I don't know if that's such a great place for him.'

'It's not usually too bad. Amy likes some of the old ladies. They show her all their pictures on their little dressers. She wants to have doilies in her room, now. And she loves Flozell. I'll give them money to buy soda from the machines. They'll be all right. I'll just be a couple hours, and then I'll take them out for dinner. Pizza, or whatever they want. I need to be back before Sarah gets home, around seven.'

'Yeah,' Alice says. 'Okay. That might be good. Thank you.'

'It's all right. It's the least I can do. You know that.'

'Can you koop him a little longer than seven?'

'Sure. Till when?'

'I don't know. Till he's twenty or so.'

'No problem.'

'I didn't think so.' She tries to smile, but it doesn't work. It just looks like she's smelling something bad.

Ted leans into Jay's room, waves at me. 'Hi, there.'

'Oh. Ted. Hello.' It feels strange to see him; it's been a while. I feel as though I need to meet him all over again.

'How long are you going to be here?'

I look at my watch. 'Another forty-five minutes or so.'

'Save five minutes for me?'

I don't like how he has said this. It's creepy. Greasy. Like the married guy at the water cooler, wearing a bad suit and flirting with all the single women. But I nod okay.

'I'll be in Jeannie's room.'

'Yes, all right. I'll come and get you.'

'How is he?' Ted asks, perfunctorily.

'Much better,' I say. Coldly. I'm not sure why. These visits to this place, they pull your emotions taut as violin strings. Sometimes the damage shows up in unexpected ways.

After he leaves, I say, 'That was Ted, Jay. I told you about him. Sometimes I like him, but sometimes I just don't. You know.'

I hear the rattle of the food cart going down the hall. 'You should wake up now,' I tell him. 'You'd get to have some wonderful nursing-home food. Chicken à la king. Chipped beef. God. Who likes that stuff? Well, your mom does. Remember when I first came to meet your parents and we had chicken à la king for lunch? I don't think I ever told you, but I went upstairs and threw up afterward. Very quietly. It wasn't because the food was that bad. It's just that I was so nervous. And then I stood in your parents' bathroom looking at their mouthwash, which wasn't the kind I used, and thinking I was all wrong for you, they'd never approve. Your mom had some really expensive perfume sitting out there, Joy, I think it was, and I picked it up and the scent got on my hands and I was terrified she'd notice it and look at your dad and raise an eyebrow, be telling him you'd brought home a thief. I washed my hands about six times to get rid of the smell. Then I came out and passed by your old bedroom. I went in and I was looking at your single bed against the wall, at the little square window above it. I was thinking about all the times you woke up there in the morning, and at night too – to get a drink, maybe, or from bad dreams. What did your mother do when you had bad dreams, Jay? How did she help you?' I wait, then say, 'Jay? What should I do?'

I take a drink of water from the glass at his

bedside, stroke the side of his face. Then, putting my fingers inside his slightly clenched fist, I try something. In a clear, authoritative voice, I say, 'Squeeze my hand if you can hear me, Jay.' I have never tried this before. It seemed too obvious. 'Just give a little squeeze,' I say. Nothing. 'You won't have to do anything else, I promise. Just do that, so I know you hear me, can you?'

I wait a moment; again, nothing. The feeling is that of standing in the middle of a large, white room with a high ceiling. It is soundless there. And then the walls recede, and the ceiling rises, and the room gets bigger and bigger and bigger. And there I am, a dot of a person, standing in the middle, doing nothing.

I blink, clear my throat. 'That's okay,' I say. 'You just listen. That's fine. What were we talking about? Oh yes. Your bedroom. Right. On the wall there was that plaque you made in Cub Scouts, using little white letters like in alphabet soup, you'd shown it to me when we took a quick tour of the house. But then when I was alone I looked at it really carefully and thought about how your hands put all the letters there, lined them up so neatly. And I was wondering if you had your uniform on when you made it, if you had that little hat on, if you were hoping really hard your mom would tell you it was wonderful. And right then I thought if I didn't marry you and have children with you, I'd die. I just had to have you. And I never regretted it, never regretted marrying you, even when we fought. Did you, Jay? I really never did. Your parents call every Sunday. I tell them you're going to be fine, that it's just a long process.'

Gloria comes into the room, nods wearily at me. She's tired today, stayed up late last night, she told me, visiting with friends who'd come to dinner. Pork tenderloin, she'd made, stuffed with prunes and lemons. That surprised me. It didn't seem like the right recipe for her. I told her that and she said, 'Suppose I told you we had collard greens with it, sweet potato pie. That make you feel better?'

'I didn't mean that,' I said.

'Yeah,' she said. 'Uh-huh.'

I'd imagined her in a silky print dress, too, dark green, as a matter of fact, pulling the roast from the oven. I'd imagined her at a dark wood dining-room table, set with her good dishes, a pastel floral pattern. I'd seen her smiling and talking, passing the butter. I didn't tell her that.

Gloria pulls Jay's covers down. Then she snaps a rubber glove on her hand, squeezes lubricant onto her fingers.

'What's up?' I say.

She shows me a suppository, one eyebrow raised at the aptness of my question.

'I'll come back,' I tell Jay. I do hope he's aware, but only selectively.

Big dog, sniffing at the back of me. I push his great head away. He puts it back. Stop. Whose dog is this? Outside in the darkness, the smell of summer around me, cut lawns, the honeysuckle, perfect open offering. I am barefoot, the concrete rough beneath my feet. Gray ripples, tiny craters. Here, the yelling of the children playing, I can't see them, it's too dark, but I hear them; and the fireflies, there they are, the moving bright lights, they flick on, they flick off. There. The shore.

Ted is sitting at the side of Jeannie's bed, his forehead against the side rail, his eyes closed. He startles when I call his name, then smiles.

'Break room?' I whisper.

'Yeah, sure.'

I expect we might find the kids there, but see them instead when we pass by the day room. They are standing before Flozell, being entertained by his card tricks. I tell them where I'll be, and they barely listen. They don't want to know where the adult is; they want to be awestruck.

Last time Amy was at the nursing home, she spent a little time alone with Flozell in the day room. He played Go Fish with her, then showed her some tricks. When we were driving home, she told me she'd asked him why he was there. I'd never felt comfortable enough to do that, but I'd always wanted to know. 'So what did he say?' I asked.

'Diarrhea of the foot.' She spoke loudly and clearly, as though she were giving a lecture in a white coat, pointing to a chart.

I thought for a minute, then asked, 'You mean diabetes?'

'Oh yeah,' she said. 'That was it. Diabetes.'

'Of the *foot*?' I said, and Amy said *yes*, that was what he'd *said*, he had diabetes of the *foot*. I could tell she was beginning to regret sharing what she'd found out with me, so I didn't ask any more questions. I didn't know if Flozell tried to explain his condition in language Amy would under-stand, or if that is his belief about what he has. The next day, I'd asked Wanda and she said Flozell had a chronically infected ulcer on his foot, huge, that he just wouldn't take care of at home. Plus he constantly cheated on his diet at home – and in the nursing home, if they didn't watch him. They found candy wrappers in his drawer. Snickers, Butterfingers. When Wanda once confronted him, Flozell said that there was a Time/Life book that would explain to her ignorant self how it was all right for diabetics to eat candy, as long as they drank enough water. 'We'll heal him up, send him home, and then see him come back again,' Wanda said. 'Believe me. I know these types.'

Ted and I get some coffee from the machine, sit opposite each other at a table in the corner. 'I haven't seen you for a while,' I say. 'I guess we've been coming at different times.'

'Yeah, I guess,' he says. And then, 'Well, I haven't been coming quite as much.'

'Oh.'

'I can't . . . Jesus, you know, I just don't think I can do this anymore. Come every day, aching for her to wake up, seeing that she doesn't and she doesn't and she doesn't.'

I stare into my coffee.

'Lainey, I've gotten involved with someone else.'

'Uh-huh.' I don't look up. I don't want to be here anymore. Where is my purse? I shift my feet, feel it beside me.

'Do you think that's terrible?'

'No!' I say. And then, looking up at him, 'I don't know, Ted. What do you want me to say?'

'I just need to talk to someone, Lainey. I guess it's awful, what I'm doing. But this woman knows if Jeannie wakes up, it's all over. She knows that. She just . . . she cooks at my house sometimes, she makes dinner for us and we . . . It's a kind of service, you know? She's lonely; I'm lonely. It's like that.'

'If it feels okay to you, Ted, then I guess it's okay for you. For me, I . . . just wouldn't do it.'

'But for how long? Jeannie's not going to wake up, Lainey. I love her. I love the memory of her. But she's not going to wake up.'

'Who said that? Did Pat Swanson tell you that? Who told you that?'

'God, who hasn't?'

'Well, you don't have to accept it. I don't accept it about Jay. I believe he will wake up.'

'Maybe he will. He doesn't have the same kind of injury that Jeannie does. They never did promise me anything, but I kept hoping . . .'

I know what Ted wants. He wants a woman who has seen his wife to say she forgives him his need for another woman. I'm not sure I have that much generosity in me.

184

'Do you talk to Jeannie?' I ask.

'Yes.' He sighs. 'Well, not so much anymore. I don't know what to say anymore. I'm so . . . amazingly tired, Lainey.'

I nod, and suddenly I'm not mad at him anymore. 'I know,' I say. 'I'm tired too. When you get that tired, you get sort of crazy, don't you think? I mean, I've been – well, I've been . . .'

He waits, and I hear myself say quietly, 'I've been hallucinating.'

'Oh, don't worry, I've done that,' he says. 'I've seen Jeannie lots of times. She passes through rooms, I see her in the corners, I hear her voice, I feel her beside me in bed. She touches the back of my neck, I swear I feel her fingers there.'

'I haven't seen Jay. But I feel his presence. I mean, I feel him there when I talk to him.'

'Do you really?'

'Yes.'

He sighs. 'I wish so hard I would. But when I talk to her, I feel as though I'm standing in front of the ocean, throwing out words to nothing.'

'Maybe you're just so exhausted—'

'No,' he says. 'It's been like that since this first happened. I've never felt she heard me since the day she came back from her surgery. I don't feel any connection. And I feel so guilty, I feel like I'm just doing it wrong. But I don't know what to do. I feel like my life has no balance. I feel desperate, I just—' He stops, looks at me, waiting. Asking. Say the handcuffs he wore were visible. They'd be made of flesh.

All right. All right. 'So what does she make you for dinner?' I ask. 'Is she a good cook?' I lean back to listen. I know that my job is to tell him it's all right and I intend to do that. Next time will be my turn. Next time, I'll ask him if what I'm doing is all right: listening to a ghost woman talk, seeing her everywhere in my house. Maybe he'll say, 'Seeing ghosts, having affairs, what's the difference? It's all to do the same thing, isn't it? It's all to get from ten o'clock to eleven.'

On the way out, I collect the kids from the day room. Flozell wheels along behind them. 'Thanks for baby-sitting again,' I tell him.

'That's all right,' he says. 'I like kids. It's when they older you got trouble. These kids told me they ain't about to grow up. We friends for life.'

'Good,' I say.

'How's Jay?'

'Oh, he's . . . you know, he's about the same.'

'Can I meet him?'

'Can you meet him?'

'That's what I heard myself say.'

'Well, he . . . I mean, he doesn't exactly respond.'

'Yeah, I know. But I like to say a few words to him. Why don't you take me there. Just be a minute.'

I say nothing, and then he tells the kids, 'Y'all wait here. We be right back.' He begins wheeling quickly down the hall toward Jay's room. When he arrives, he waits for me outside the door.

'I don't know,' I say.

'Just let me come in a minute. Introduce us.'

I look into Flozell's face, see a kind of honest earnestness I haven't witnessed outside of children. 'Oh, all right,' I say. 'Come on.'

Flozell follows me in, wheels up to the side of the bed. Jay is on his back, hands arranged over his stomach. 'Jay,' I say. 'There's someone here I'd like you to meet. Who'd like to meet you. This is Flozell.' I turn to Flozell, say quietly, 'I'm sorry. I forgot your last name.'

'Smith,' he says, disgustedly. 'How you forget that?'

'Sorry,' I say, and then, to Jay, 'Flozell Smith.'

A little moment, and then Flozell wheels closer, takes Jay's hand. 'My man,' he says, gently. And then says nothing, just stays there, looking into Jay's face. I step back, look at the massive hulk of Flozell holding the thinning hand of my husband, and I want to weep. I cannot for the life of me say the particular reason why.

When I come home, Ed is sitting on the porch. I nod at him, start to walk past. 'Lainey?'

'Yeah!' My voice is brittle with brightness.

'Want to take a walk?'

'Well, you know, I just got home.'

'Just for a few minutes.'

I want to say how difficult this would be, but it wouldn't be. It's still early. Amy and Timothy are at his house. Sarah won't be home for another half hour.

'All right,' I say. 'Just let me tell Alice.'

'She knows.'

Great. 'Oh. Well, then.'

He stands up, tucks his shirt in.

'I'll just put my purse away,' I say. 'It's too heavy.'

'Right.'

I go inside, notice the message light blinking, play it back with my hands clenched into fists. It's only Dolly. I push the save button, stop listening. Later.

Just before I go out the door, I think about calling Alice, to whisper, This is it. We're going for a walk. Want me to say anything in particular? I almost do, but then decide no, I'll talk to her later. After it's over.

I close the door behind me, smile falsely at Ed as we walk down the porch steps. I have an awful sensation, much like that of being disappointed by a blind date. In situations like this, the core that is your real self stays behind, feeling sorry for you, waiting for you to come back and reenter yourself.

'Don't be so nervous,' Ed says.

'I'm not!'

He looks at me.

'Well, I mean . . . Okay. Fine.'

Nothing for a little while, except the soft sound of our shoes on the sidewalk. I notice that I am thirty-five years old and still avoid the cracks. I hope my mother appreciates this.

'I thought maybe the park,' Ed says.

'Well, I was thinking more . . . you know, just around the block. I need to return some calls. I have to get back.'

We pass a bus stop, and Ed gestures toward the bench. 'Can we just sit here for a minute?'

I sit down, turn expectantly toward him.

'You know what I want to talk about, right?'

'I guess.'

'I'm not doing what she thinks, Lainey.'

I nod.

'I'm really not.'

'Okay.'

'I get . . . I don't know, removed, sometimes. I know that. I'm kind of hard to reach. But it's just a mood. I'm not seeing anyone. I love Alice.'

'Uh-huh.'

'I'd like you to try to help me, Lainey. I don't want her to think there's someone else.'

'Well. I kind of think that's your job, Ed.'

'But she doesn't believe me!'

'I have to tell you, Ed. I'm really uncomfortable about this whole thing. I mean, talking to you. I don't know what to say. I don't know what to tell you. Alice thinks you're having an affair. I asked how she knew and she said she could just tell. She didn't give me any details.'

'All right, I've been working more hours. That's the only thing.'

'She didn't say that.'

'She doesn't know that. I don't want her to know that. She doesn't know where I've been. I'm . . . Listen, Lainey, I know you're good friends. But I have to tell you something now that I don't want you to tell her.'

'I don't think I can promise you that.'

'Please. Listen. I'm working more hours for a reason. It's . . . It's because I want to save enough so we can buy a house. She really wants a house, and I've almost got enough. I want to surprise her. That's all.'

'I see.' I don't think Alice wants a house. She

190

would have told me. She likes where she lives. She wouldn't even move to the farm.

'All right?'

'Yes, all right.'

'So can you sort of . . . I don't know, can you just tell her that I'm not involved with another woman? I swear it's true. I swear it. I don't want her to . . . I don't want her to have to suffer like this.'

'I don't think she's *suffering*, Ed.'

'Well, I think she is.'

He's right, of course. I just don't want him to know it. I want him to think her broken heart is the equivalent of a hangnail, that losing him will be a passing inconvenience like having to switch laundry detergents. What is this talk for? What can he be thinking? That I'll walk back to the house and invite Alice over and defend him because he told me to?

'Ed?' I hate his name. I hate the name Ed. It's too short. The letters are ugly together. The name sounds like you're starting to say something and a fishbone catches in your throat. That's what I'll tell Alice, that we had a talk and I hate his stupid name.

'Why do you love Alice?' I ask.

'Pardon?'

'I said, "Why do you love Alice?"'

He laughs. 'Well, why do you?'

'That's not the question.'

'Well, I . . . I think that's kind of personal, Lainey. Frankly, I find it odd that you ask.'

'Never mind,' I say. 'Sorry.' I find it odd that he can't answer. Alice is right. He's lying.

The message is from Dolly, asking me to call her on Monday, she's got an idea for me. A plan for working at home. That's not a bad idea. It's May already. I think Jay's benefits decrease dramatically mid-month. I've got to find out. I've been thinking it's beside the point, what the benefits are. But maybe it's not. Maybe I'd better find out about long-range benefits. Maybe I'd better see if Frank can let me work full-time. Maybe Jay will lie there and lie there and lie there and lie there. Or not. Maybe he will not keep lying there. Maybe he'll die. Is this it? Is this the time just before I become a widow working full-time at Beverage World, finding gray hairs at my temples one morning and turning from the bathroom mirror to show no one? I hear the screen door bang shut and I'm so glad Amy's home. I will ask her to sit on my lap and I will braid her hair. Things like that help, when you feel suddenly made of glass, when if it weren't for your sorrow you'd start screaming.

Ten fifty-five. The kids are in bed, asleep, I think. I don't want to check because if they're not asleep I don't have the energy to do anything about it. I made Amy go to the bathroom twice before bed. I'm tired of her wetting the bed. The second time, I leaned against the doorjamb, watching her, and heard Evie's voice in my ear. 'A teaspoon of honey will help her. It'll attract and hold the fluid. She'll wake up dry.' And here is the dream world I live in now: when Amy came out of the bathroom, I brought her down into the kitchen with me and gave her a teaspoon of honey as though the pediatrician had called me, saying, 'You know what works?'

'Why do I have to take this?' Amy asked.

'To help you sleep,' I said. And then Sarah, who was at the table watching, said, 'What about me?' and I gave her a teaspoon, too. Couldn't hurt. My children love taking medicine, even when it tastes terrible. It's very unusual. I worry about it. They probably can't wait to grow up and be hypochondriacs.

Now I make myself a cup of tea, sit at the kitchen table, look across from me and here she is again, her simultaneously vague and too-real presence.

'Go away,' I say, so quietly I'm not sure I've said it.

She stares at me with a calm kind of compassion, and I put my hands over my face, squeeze my eyes shut hard.

I hear a noise and look up, expecting her to be over at the sink, doing something useful. But it is not Evelyn Arlene Benson, ghost of a woman who lived here and now does not – but does anyway. It is Alice, letting herself in the back door.

'I saw your light,' she says, sitting down.

I nod, then remember that I haven't spoken to her since I talked to Ed. 'So. You ready?'

She nods.

'You want me to tell the truth?'

193

She nods again.

'I think he's . . . I think you're right.'

'Did he say anything about her?'

'No. He denied it.'

'How? What did he say, exactly?'

I think for a moment, and realize that I don't remember. There is a point at which a muscle simply will not work any longer, and I feel as though my brain is like that lately, that what I need is to let it alone for a good long while.

'That bad, huh?' Alice says.

'No, it's . . . You know, Alice, I'm having a hard time remembering. I've been having some things happen that make me think . . . Well, never mind. I remember. He said he was being distant, he knew that. He said he does that sometimes. But that he isn't seeing anyone. He's just working more. He wants to save money to . . . Well, he wants to buy you something. That's what he said. He's working more to buy you something and he's not fooling around. And oh, he loves you.'

'He said that?'

'Yes.'

She chews at her lip, thinks a little. Then, 'Buy what? What's he going to buy?'

'Well, I don't know if I should tell you, Alice. I mean, what if he's telling the truth?'

'Then I'll be happy.'

'I don't know.'

'Tell me.'

'All right, fine. He said he was going to buy you a house. That you wanted a house.'

194

Quiet, except for the low hum of the refrigerator. She looks frozen, staring off into space.

'Alice?'

She looks at me.

'Is it true?'

'You know, Lainey, I wonder if it would be all right with God if we exchanged situations. If we could have Ed in that bed instead of Jay. Because that would make some sense. Wouldn't it?'

I say nothing.

'Maybe I could go home and bonk him on the head a little, do you think?'

'Alice, I'm sorry.'

'You know, what's really insulting is that he uses that. A house. I never wanted to own a house. I mean, couldn't he have said . . . I don't know, a car? A car, that would actually run? That doesn't make weird noises all the time? It's an insult to say I want a house when I love living here so much. I love it here! I love duplexes, I love having you as a neighbor, I love our big front porch and the wood trim we have that you can't find anymore and the size of our kitchens and the wide sidewalks out front. I love that we can walk to the store and the little library. I love that this house is so old, that there's such a strong sense of other lives that have been here.'

At this, I start listening even harder. But she stops talking.

When I turn out the light for sleep that night, I close my eyes and, as I often do, remember how it used to be when I didn't sleep alone. This seems to be painful necessity, the way the tongue seeks out the sore in the mouth. I close my eyes, think of the pleasure it was to back up to Jay, to feel his arm around my middle, his face against the back of my neck. Everything was in place when we lay together that way. I knew I was home. His smell was a kind of blanket to me. Safety. I notice that I still stay on my side of the bed, leaving room for him. If this goes on for years, will I still do that? If this goes on for years, will there ever be a point at which I am able to laugh with all of myself? It doesn't seem so. And if that's true, if my spirit must stay forever restrained because his is, wouldn't it be better if he died? Maybe it would be. It would be cleaner. And after a while, perhaps even easier.

I sit up, turn on the light. I want to know the thing I should say *stop* to, the thing I can tell *I didn't mean that*. I didn't mean that. I put my hand to my mouth, rock back and forth. I didn't mean it.

Wednesday morning, I am putting on lipstick, getting ready to go to the nursing home, when I hear the front door open. 'Lainey?' Alice calls.

'In the bathroom,' I yell, and then stand back, look to see if I stayed in the lines for once.

Alice sticks her head in. 'Hi.'

'Hi.'

'Are you leaving?'

'Yeah. Why?'

'Could you do something for me first?'

Her voice is different than usual. I turn around to face her. 'What's up?' I have a sudden and terrible feeling she is going to tell me she's pregnant and wants me to go with her to have an abortion. It's that kind of face, full of conflict. But what she says is, 'I want to go to her house.'

'Whose house?'

'You know.'

'*Her* house?'

'Yeah.'

'You want to meet her?'

'She's not home.'

'So why do you want to go to her house?'

'I just want to see it.'

'Alice—'

'Don't – *tell* me anything. I want to see it. I have to see it. Don't say anything about it. Just come with me.'

'Well, how do you even know where it is? How do you know *who* she is?'

'I found out.'

'How?'

'I followed him. After work. Last night when Timothy ate dinner at your house? I followed Ed when he left work.'

'Oh, Alice.'

'No! I wanted to see. For sure.'

'And?'

'And he went into a town house and came out about forty minutes later, looking . . . happy. And with a wet head from a shower.'

'Well, then you saw her house already.'

'No, you don't understand. I want to see it *slowly*. I want to look in the windows. I want to see her furniture.'

I turn out the bathroom light, walk past her. 'Come and sit down with me, Alice.'

'No! Listen, Lainey. I know what I'm doing. I have my reasons. I'm asking you to come with me. I need someone to . . . help me. To watch for people to come.' This last she says in a lowered voice, looking down. Apparently she knows how she's sounding.

'Alice,' I say gently. 'Won't this just make you feel worse?'

She looks up. 'Of course. That's the point.'

'Oh,' I say. 'All right.' I get it. Sometimes, just when you think you're going to die from pain, rage steps in to save you. There's only so much room in a human heart. Thank God.

The town house is a tasteful gray structure with white trim, located in the arty part of town. There's a pot of red geraniums on the little front porchette. The unit is an end one, toward the back of the complex. My job as lookout won't be too hard. Alice goes up to the front door, reads the brass nameplate. 'S. Hermann,' she says.

'Ugh,' I say. 'It's probably "Suzanne." I hate "Suzanne."'

'It's probably "Slut."' Alice opens her wallet, takes something out, slides it in the crack of the door and up, and the door opens.

'Alice!'

She turns around, startled. 'It works!'

'How did you do that?' I say. '*Stop* that!'

'Come here, come here!' she whispers. 'Let's go in!'

'Alice, you can't do this! What if she's home?'

Alice leans in, says, 'Hello?' Then, looking back at me, 'She's not home. She's at work, fucking my husband in the supply closet.' She goes in the front door.

I stand still for a moment, then follow her, close the door behind me. Alice is standing in the living room, staring at a painting over a sofa. It's hypermodern, as is everything else in the room.

'How did you get in?' I whisper. And then, 'We have to get out of here!'

Alice stares at the painting while she answers me. 'A friend of mine told me about this a long time ago. She said if the dead bolt wasn't on, you could slide a credit card in and open the door. She's right.'

'Fine. Now you've seen the place. Let's go.' Alice doesn't move. I see a flowering floor plant in one corner, a beautiful burgundy throw over an armchair. Slut has a lot of books, a whole wall of them. Very nice. From the living room, I can see part of the kitchen. I tiptoe toward it.

'Where are *you* going?' Alice whispers.

'I just . . . let me see the kitchen.'

Alice follows me into a small room, nicely equipped. 'Wow,' I say. 'Look at her appliances. She has *every*thing.' I start to pull open a drawer.

'Don't do that,' Alice says.

'Why not?'

'I don't know. An alarm might go off.'

'*Now* you think of that. If she doesn't arm her door, I'm sure she doesn't arm her kitchen drawer.' I pull it open. 'Look, she has good knives, too.'

'Come on,' Alice says. 'Let's find the bedroom. That's what I really want to see. Or do you want to inspect her spices?'

I do, actually. She probably has the mail-order

vanilla, whole nutmeg that she grates on a special fifteen-dollar grater. But I follow Alice into the bedroom. I pass a bathroom on the way, see blue pottery on the tank top, blue and white towels rolled up in a basket beside the tub, what looks like a silk kimono hanging on a hook. A small vase by the sink holds one white freesia.

In the bedroom, there's a kind of Chinese motif – a lot of black lacquer and red. Alice uses a brass pull to open the drawer of the bedside stand and I lean over her shoulder to see in. There's a pair of glasses in there, a tasteful tortoiseshell; a tube of generic hand lotion, a paperback book of poetry and a large number of condoms. 'Oh God,' I say. 'Come on, Alice. Shut that. Don't look.'

Alice closes the drawer slowly, stands still for a long, terrible moment. 'I just want to see her clothes,' she says. 'And then we'll leave.'

She starts toward the closet and then stops, stares at a sweater lying across a chair in the corner. 'Look,' she says, pointing at it.

'What?' I say.

'That's Ed's.'

'Are you sure?'

Alice goes to pick the sweater up. 'Yeah. I bought it for him.' She smells it, holds her face against it for a while. 'Nice new cologne.' She looks up, her face remarkably impassive. 'Let's go,' she says.

I follow her out. On the porch, she touches the largest blossom on the geranium. I think she's going to pinch it off, but she leaves it there.

I come home before the kids, meet them on the porch when they come back from school. Alice doesn't need to do anything extra today. I give them the candy bars I bought on the way home because I know if I give them those they'll do whatever I say for the next hour. I tell them to eat outside, then to play for a while. And then I go over to Alice's. She is in the kitchen, sitting before an empty cup. I think she's probably been sitting there a long time. She looks up, smiles at me.

'So?' I say.

'So I'll be a single mother. It's all the rage.'

'You're going to separate?'

She shrugs. 'Yeah. That's what I want to do. I think it might be better, anyway. It's hard, to be lonely in a marriage. Especially when you try to act as though you're not lonely. You know, every weekend morning I'd get up before Ed, and I'd make coffee and I'd hope that he would come down and sit with me, that it would be early morning and we'd be sitting in the kitchen together, having coffee and talking. It seems like once you have kids that's such a rare thing. But he would never get up, even the few times that I asked him the night before and he promised that he would. I'd wait, and the coffee would get stale and when he got up he'd throw it out and make a new pot. And I always thought that was so sad, you know, that two people who lived together in the same house would be making separate pots of coffee. Do you know what I mean?'

'I know what you mean.' There would be an island of sun on the kitchen table, warming the bananas in the fruit bowl. Jay and I would be in our pajamas, teeth unbrushed, faces still creased with sleep, yawning, ignoring the paper in favor of describing our dreams, talking about what we might do that day, wondering if we had any money we could go throw around. I knew it was a rare thing every time it happened; I am not unaware of what happens on most Sunday mornings when the people have been married for a while, when they are past the time of lounging on love seats, looking cute in their T-shirt pajamas and sweatsocks and glasses, the woman resting her feet in the lap of the man as they read the paper. I know how uncommon it is for the interest to hold, the joy. Before I met Jay, I worked one summer as a waitress. An old man came in with his wife, taking her out to dinner on their anniversary. When I brought their salads, he told me they'd been married fifty-three years. Then he took her hand and they looked at each other with such honest and tremulous affection I had to go in the back room where the potatoes and onions were kept so I could weep. It was because I knew it was possible, that sort of staying power, and I was afraid I'd never find it. But I did.

Alice sighs hugely, then looks up at me. 'Would you say that you're happy? I mean, before the accident. Were you happy?'

I want to say no. It seems disloyal not to. She's feeling so badly. I ought to keep her company. But I tell her the truth. I nod yes.

'But . . . would you say you're a happy person anyway? I mean, you know, optimistic?'

'I guess so.'

'I'm just trying . . . I just would like to know some things about you, Lainey. About your nature. I'm just trying to figure some things out, here.'

'Well, yes, I would say I was optimistic.'

'So you look forward to the future.'

'It's been hard lately.'

'I know. I know that. But I mean, generally.'

'Yes. Yes, Alice, I do! Okay?'

'Well, don't get mad.'

'I'm not.'

'Yes, you are.'

'I'm not! It's just that . . . I don't know, it's kind of a sore spot with me. People make fun of me for . . . Okay, I had a roommate my first year in college who was depressed all the time. I think she was majoring in depression. But she was very

205

chic, everybody thought she was very hip. She dressed only in black, dyed her hair black, wore this thick line of black makeup around her eyes, even to bed. Black panties, black bra, black socks, black shoes . . . you know. She never smiled. And I really irritated her. We got a bottle of wine one night and got drunk in our room and she asked what I felt like first thing in the morning. She said to tell the truth, now, tell the truth. She was talking in this really low voice, her head close to mine. So I said, in this really low voice back, that I felt happy first thing in the morning. She sat there for a long time, kind of swaying, and then she said, "You feel *happy*." And I said yes. And she said, Why? And I said I didn't know, exactly, but that for one thing I was very interested to see what might happen. She said, "You mean, you feel, a sense of . . . ex*cite*ment?" and I said yes, that was what it was. She said, *"Really,"* and I said yes, really.

'The next morning I was standing at the window in my underwear and a T-shirt, watching the sun come up. She told me I had a rip in my underwear, and I said yes I knew that but these were my period pants, I used them the first day of my period, and she said she thought that was ridiculous. Sad. She pulled the covers back over her head and went to sleep. I got dressed and went out for breakfast. It was a fine day, a bit of cold in the air, frost on the grass. I had two over easy and hash browns at Al's Diner and the coffee was so perfect I drank too much and then I talked too much in humanities class. When I got back to the room, it was one-thirty and my roommate was just getting up. And we just looked at each other, and I know she was thinking I was such a jerk and I said, "Look. For me, the glass is a fucking waterfall. Get used to it."'

Alice is staring at me. I can't tell how she feels. 'I know,' I say. 'I'm an imbecile.'

'You're not an imbecile,' Alice says. 'It's something else. Naïveté, maybe. But that's only part of it. I envy you. I mean, you're the kind of person who gets happy if the leftovers fit exactly into the Tupperware container.'

I say nothing.

'Right?'

'No,' I say. But I'm lying. I do get a little charge when everything fits.

'It's all right,' Alice says. 'I admire you. I think you've got a good way of thinking.'

Not always. Not lately. 'Alice?' I say. 'I have to tell you something. I think things are starting to fall apart on me. My mind, I mean. I feel sort of shaky. I've been having these thoughts . . .'

She stands, holds out her hand. 'Come on. Let's go out in the backyard. Tell me out there. It's nice outside.'

We go outside and settle ourselves in the grass. I can hear the kids' voices on the other side of the house.

'So what's going on?' Alice says.

'Do you remember reading some old letters that were here in the basement?' I ask.

'No. What letters?'

'You know, from the woman who used to live here.'

'No. Are there letters down there?'

'Yeah,' I say. Maybe Alice wasn't with me. Maybe I read them alone. 'Never mind,' I say. 'I just . . . I've been feeling sort of crazy.'

'You'd be crazy not to,' Alice says. She lies down, closes her eyes. 'Did you know that Ed never proposed to me? I did it. I asked him. Twice.'

'Did you?'

'He was on the rebound, he'd just been dumped by somebody. I never met her. I'm so sorry he said yes.'

'Oh, Alice, maybe it's just a bad time. You know? Maybe you'll work it out. People do.'

'No. Now that I know what's going on for sure, I can't wait for him to leave. Really.'

'Right,' I say. And then, because I don't believe her and we need to move on to something else, I say, 'I'm ready for the hot weather. I can't wait for the kids to run through the sprinkler. I can't wait to run through the sprinkler myself.'

'Me neither,' Alice says. And then, 'You know, it's funny that you should mention those letters. Today, I was sitting at the kitchen table feeling really terrible and I all of a sudden started thinking about the people who might have first lived in this house. And I had this vision of a woman. She was sitting at the table in the kitchen with her kids. There was a tablecloth, and a fan

208

on the table turning from side to side, and she and the kids were playing a game with those wooden markers, drinking lemonade, the old-fashioned kind that looks white. She had on a sleeveless blouse and a skirt, all ironed, remember ironing? And the boy was wearing this striped T-shirt and the little girl a dress with a bow that tied in the back. It was so clear, everything!'

Every hair on the back of my neck is raised. 'You saw this?' I ask. 'I mean, literally?'

Alice leans up on one elbow, looks at me. 'No! What do you think? No, I just saw it in my head. It was just a little daydream. Nice diversion, though. Took my mind off things for a minute.'

No it wasn't a daydream, I think. But I don't say anything. Potato salad was in the refrigerator, hamburger shaped into patties and ready to get fried. The woman straightened her back, stretched it, when the game was over. She had a mild ache between her shoulder blades, a good kind of fatigue. She moved to the sink to slice tomatoes while the kids put away the game, looked up at the clock, got glad.

Monday morning, when I get to Jay's room, I find Gloria straightening his sheets. She must have just bathed him; his hair is slicked back in a way he would never comb it.

'Anything new?' I ask. Gloria shakes her head.

'Okay.' I lower the bed rail, sit beside him, kiss his cheek.

Lainey. Your flesh smell. The small breeze of you bending over me.

'He had one eye open today, like to scare me to death,' Gloria says.

I look at Jay's face.

'Just a reflex. He wasn't seeing nothing. I shut it again,' Gloria says.

No.

'He can't be doing that, he'll get an infection. You tell me if you see it open again; I'll tape it shut.'

'His eyes? You'd tape his eyes shut?'

'It doesn't hurt. You put a little dressing there, some tape over it.'

'But what if he wakes up? He won't be able to see.'

'He wakes up, he'll rip it off. Take it right off.'

'All right,' I say, though it isn't.

'What'd you bring him today?' Gloria asks. I suppose it's amusing to the staff, the things I do every time I come here. But they show me a certain amount of respect, too. Most of them.

'You want to know what I brought?'

'Show me.'

'Okay.' I open my purse, show Gloria small plastic bags, knotted with rubber bands.

'Dope?' she asks, incredulously.

'No,' I tell her. 'Spices.'

'Spices.'

'Yes.'

She straightens, nods. 'Uh-huh.'

'Where's Wanda today?' I ask. Wanda would say, 'Spices! Great!'

'She's on nights this week. Working the moonlight shift. And there's a full moon tonight. I feel sorry for her, all hell breaks out nights when the moon is full. Mrs Eliot be screaming her lungs out all night long, I can guarantee you that. That woman's evil, one of those old ladies be squinting out the window from behind the curtains, don't let no kids come on her lawn. "Git on out of here, now, don't you be stepping on my grass!" You know what I mean. She takes the balls away from the children, keeps them in her creepy old basement.'

'Oh, come on.'

'It's the God's truth. Her daughter told me. Mean woman, her whole life long. Used to wear her daughter out she come home one minute late. She pinches you every time you give her a bath. Hard! One time I'm washing her leg and she kicks me in the stomach. I nearly laid her out flat. I'm telling you, they say respect the patient, respect the patient, but that's hard to do when they trying to kill you.'

'How's Jeannie Nichols?' I ask. I haven't seen Ted since we last talked.

'Oh.' Gloria's face changes. She looks away from me to fiddle with Jay's sheets. 'She died last week. You didn't know?'

'No, I . . . Nobody told me.'

'She got pneumonia. She fried herself. Temperature off the chart the night she died. Hundred five, hundred six.'

'Was her husband here?'

'Oh yeah. He was with her the last whole day. You really didn't know?'

'No, I haven't seen Ted for a while. Do you have his phone number?'

'Yeah, I think we still got it. You want it?'

'Please.'

Gloria leaves the room and I sit still for a moment, thinking. And then I turn to Jay. 'That won't happen to you. I brought you something,

Jay. I've got some spices here. Just . . . for fun.' I put the cinnamon under his nose. 'Now, here. Isn't this nice?'

A call to the table, my mother's hands. Breakfast.

'How about this? This is sage, Jay. You know? What's this remind you of? Thanksgiving, right? You remember that turkey platter we always use, that the woman down the street threw away and we snuck out that night and got it?'

I take out the nutmeg, rub some between my fingers, hold it beneath his nose. 'Christmas, Jay. Eggnog.' I open the clove bag. 'Easter. Ham.' I keep going. I line up the little spice bags all across his chest. All across his University of California T-shirt are requests from the kitchen. Come back, says the curry, the oregano. And me. Sometimes when I'm doing this, when I'm trying really hard to reach him, I'll start to perspire. Which I've never done before. I share this with an aunt of mine, we never perspire, it's kind of a family joke about how Aunt Mary and I are too repressed to sweat. But doing this, calling Jay, I often feel a wetness come under my arms, across my forehead. And almost every time, I start to cry a little, too. I try not to let him know. Sometimes I feel so hard that he's just so close to being ready to answer me. I can feel it in me like a taut line extending from my brain to my heels. It may be what's holding me up. I don't know. I don't know anything anymore. I wish he could tell me, somehow. Even if he were to wake up for one

213

second, take hold of my wrists, look into my eyes and say, 'I can hear you, Lainey. Keep trying. It's going to take three more months.' Fine, I would say. Just so I know.

On the surface, the soft shell of skin, and I am only below here, loose, unmoored, bumping up against the sides of myself. Look deeper. The will to turn over is a handful of empty air, a concept amusing and useless. I am seeing the genius of being alive, and it holds me. I have the ear to hear now, I have the original eye, there is an understanding. I try, I think hard, use the dim light left to pull my muscles in and up, suspend myself from dropping deeper. Though it does seem soft and so welcoming. Though the black space does form a mouth calling my real name, and it is heard with such clarity I cannot yet move from listening to it. A rare directness. The source.

Gloria gave me not only Ted's number, but his address, and that is where I am now, parked on the curb in front of a smallish, modern house only about fifteen minutes from mine. There is a car in the driveway; I think he's home.

I look at myself in the rearview mirror to see if I'm ready, if I know what I want to say. What I see reflected back is a tired-looking woman with dirty-blond hair in a ponytail, who looks scared. I had a fantasy on the way over, that I would walk into Ted's kitchen, which would look remarkably like mine. There would be a storm going on in his face. He would be wearing black pants, a black turtleneck. I would sit at the kitchen table, my folded hands in my lap, my knees together, and he would pace in front of the windows, stopping occasionally to smash a pane out with his fist. I would not react too much. I would understand. When he was finished, I

215

would help bandage his hands. Drive him to the ER.

I put a little lipstick on, push back the stray hairs on the sides of my head, go up to the house. Ted answers the door almost immediately, which surprises me. 'Lainey!' he says, surprised himself, and then, 'God. How nice to see you. Come in.' He is not in black. He is wearing a plaid shirt, tucked into tan pants. The sleeves are buttoned at his wrist, and he has buttoned every button on the front, too. I believe I know something about the way he got dressed this morning. About the way he finds relief in simple activity.

We go into his kitchen, which is not like mine at all. It is mostly white, with the exception of a black stone counter. Granite, I think. It's very modern. Not particularly warm. But pretty. I sit at the kitchen table. The chair is a hard white metal, black cushion on the seat. 'Something to drink?' he asks.

'No thanks,' I say, and then, 'Ted, I want to tell you how sorry I am. About Jeannie.'

He nods, sits down with me, so purposefully mild in his movements and his manner I think he might explode. 'It was pneumonia,' he says.

'Yes, I heard.'

'Oh? Who told you?'

'Gloria.'

'They're still talking about her, then.'

'Yes, they are.'

'Well, that's good. That's good.'

'Was the funeral . . . ?'

216

'Day before yesterday. It was very odd, Lainey, picking out a dress for her to get buried in. It's odder than you think it's going to be. Not that you will. I mean, I hope you don't have to.'

I say nothing, realize I am holding my breath, exhale quietly.

'So, here I am. It's over. Which I used to wish for, you know, I used to wish it would just get over with. I would pull into the parking lot of that goddamn nursing home and I would hate it so much, I would just hate the sight of it.'

'Yes, I know.'

'I wanted it to be over with. I probably shouldn't have wanted that.'

'No one would blame you for that, Ted.'

He nods, then looks up at me. 'Something to drink?'

'No thanks.'

'I asked you that already, didn't I?'

'Yes. But that's okay. Ted, are you . . . Is there anything I can do?'

'No.'

'Is there anyone who's helping you?'

He looks up. 'There's nothing to help with. That's what's so hard. There is only her absence. I suppose it's like an illness I'll have for a while. God, Lainey, when I wake up in the middle of the night . . . I can't tell you what it's like. I have this tiny moment of not knowing what's wrong. And then this overwhelming . . .' He stops, attempts a smile. 'It's so quiet, real grief. I guess I didn't know that.'

I open my purse, write my phone number down on a piece of paper, slide it across the table to him. The numbers look so black against the white. 'Just in case you want to call,' I say. 'You can call any time. Really.'

'Uh-huh,' he says. 'Okay. Thanks, Lainey.' He folds the paper into fours and puts it in his pocket. 'I think . . . You know, I hope you don't mind, Lainey, but I don't think I'm quite ready to talk to anyone. I'm sorry.'

'Oh, no, it's . . . *I'm* sorry. I should have called. I just wanted to tell you, you know . . .' I stand up, slide my purse over my shoulder. 'Okay, so . . .'

'Yes,' he says. 'All right.'

I let myself out. What I know is that I will never, ever see him again. I'd thought we might embrace when I left. Somehow.

What I want, on the drive home, is to not think of anything. Of course this does not happen. I think, what outfit would I pick out for Jay? What would I do with the rest of his clothes? What would I do with the kit for the diesel airplane he was going to build? When I came home from the funeral, what would I do? Ask the kids to go to their bedrooms because it would be unbearable to see him in them? And then open the refrigerator, and stand there?

I think, he was only in the middle. He didn't even have a chance to say good-bye. Isn't it better if you get a chance to say good-bye? And then I think, maybe not. Maybe it's better if it's sudden and you don't suffer. But maybe he's suffering now. How would I know?

I put my hand up to my face. I pinch my cheek, to feel something else. It doesn't work. I pinch my chin, my ear. It doesn't work. I turn on the radio, then turn it off.

How foolish to think as often as I do that the force of my will can save him. But I can't help it. It's human nature. It's because, once catastrophe has occurred, we expect our lives to behave. We accept the Awful Event because we have to. But after that, we would like our lives to follow a certain order, a design of our own making. This seems like reasonable compensation. This seems like what ought to happen. Only it hardly ever does.

I accelerate to make a yellow light, think about a friend of mine once saying that if she hadn't met and married her husband at the time she did, she's certain she would have met and married someone else at the same exact time. I said I didn't know about that. I said I was the kind of person who, when I was a little girl, pulled kissing jacks out of the game so that they could stay together. I said I had great respect for seemingly arbitrary events.

I think of a time I'd pulled an all-nighter at college, then stayed up very late the next night, too. I had never been so exquisitely tired in my life. I felt like my hair hurt. When I finally went to bed, I wept with relief and when I woke up, the sky was a very peculiar color. I couldn't tell if it was dawn or dusk. I looked at my watch, which of course did not help me. It said 5:45, you figure out the rest. I got this terrible, panicky feeling, and I called the operator, and, feeling very silly, said, 'Can you tell me if it's night or day?' She was very kind, an older-sounding woman, and she said it was night; and then she stayed on the line to make sure I was okay. That's what Jay did for me. He was my operator. And I think I was his. I was. I was his.

I turn down my street, notice how many leaves there are now. Once I was visiting a friend whose backyard bordered an acre of woods. It was a pretty day, and we were sitting outside on the grass, talking. Suddenly it began to rain, but just in the woods. It was in isolated spots, and in only one spot at a time: here, then there, then over there. I looked up at the sky. Blue. I held out my hand. Nothing but soft summer air. I looked at the woods again and it was raining again: here, then there, then over there. I looked at my friend, puzzled, and she smiled and said, 'I know. Doesn't it look strange? It's because it rained last night and the leaves are all full of water. The squirrels jump from one bough to the other and shake it off.'

'Oh,' I said. 'It looks like it's just choosing to rain in certain places.'

'Yes,' she said. 'That's what it looks like. But that's not what it is.'

There is some comfort in that story, for the way it suggests that there is a reason for everything, even though it may not be apparent. But there is this, too: some places get to stay dry. Some places don't get hit at all. I will take my comfort there.

At home, I take exquisite care with dinner preparation. Tomatoes sliced to be the exact same size. Lettuce washed, dried, washed again. Macaroni and cheese from scratch, the big fat elbow noodles that they like, the mild cheese. I am so grateful for the presence of my children, for the soft sound of their overlapping voices in the next room. They are playing with their baby doll, making up a perfect life for her. 'Here is her bedroom, where stars live on the walls,' Amy is saying.

'Give her here,' Sarah says. 'I need to *breast*feed her.' They giggle from behind their hands; the high sound is muffled. I reach behind myself, straighten the bow on the back of my apron. Fruit salad for dessert, whipped cream piled up high. Let me just have this little island. This floe.

The next morning, after the kids have left for school, Alice lets herself in, sits down at the kitchen table.

'Hi,' I say. And then, 'What? What happened?'

She smiles, nods. 'It's not another woman.'

'Oh, Alice. Good. See? I'm glad. You talked?'

'Yup, and it's not another woman. What it is, is a man.'

I stop pouring coffee, put the mug down on the counter. 'He's . . . It's a man?'

'Late in the afternoon on the day we broke into that town house, I was putting away laundry and I found Ed's sweater in his drawer. You know, the one we'd seen in the bedroom that morning. And I thought, Wait, what *is* this? And then I thought, Oh God, I think I know what this is. I think I know what this is. When Ed came home, I confronted him. And he told me. At first he denied it, but then he sat on the edge of the bed and wept and wept and wept. And he told me. They have matching sweaters, Lainey. Isn't that cute?'

I swallow. I can't speak.

'Who should we call, Lainey? Phil or Oprah?'

'Jesus, Alice.'

'Oh. Right. I hadn't thought of Him.'

Ten-fifty at night, a weariness I can feel over me like a second skin. I've just now arrived at Jay's room because I spent the whole day and evening with Alice. We hired a sitter to come after school and we took off. We went to a bookstore, we walked in a park, we tried on bathing suits, we ate strawberry pie at the Woolworth's counter and that's the only time she started to cry. It was over quickly. 'Whoops,' she said. 'Sorry.' She wiped the tears away. 'You can cry if you want to,' I told her. And she said, 'I know. I don't want to.'

She pushed her plate away, leaned toward me. 'Do you think that every time we made love, he was wishing . . . or, you know, imagining . . . ?'

'The thought did occur to me.'

'I mean, sometimes he wanted to try . . . uh . . .'

'Greek love?' I asked, exceedingly quietly.

'What's that?'

'You know. Behind.'

She nodded.

'Well,' I said. 'I think lots of guys like to try that, whatever their orientation.'

'And I'll tell you, he *always* liked—'

'Well, they *all* like *that*,' I said, quickly.

223

The waitress came toward us with her full pot of coffee. 'Fill her up?' she asked.

Alice and I looked at each other, stifled everything.

It was in the afternoon as we waited on the porch steps for the kids to come home that Alice said, 'It's a relief in a way. You know what I mean?'

'You mean that it's not another woman?'

'Yeah. Not that it's not horrible. And it's . . . you know, complicated. God, is it complicated! But at least it's not another woman. And it explains a lot of things. There was always a kind of holding back in him that was too . . . secretive. Not just male reticence. Well, actually, maybe it *was* male reticence. But now that he's told me the truth, there's such a relief in him, and a kind of softness I never saw. I actually think I like him better now, honest. I hate him, but I like him better.'

We saw the kids rounding the corner and stopped talking, waited to examine the contents of their schoolbags: the too-long PTA notices, the lunchbox rejects, the handed-back papers. Timothy got a smiling turtle sticker for doing all his work right, which he always does. He's tired of stickers. He's suggested to Alice that his teacher might pay him. Alice has suggested that feeling good about doing work well is reward enough. Timothy has suggested that's ridiculous.

So now Alice is at my house, lying on my sofa. She'll stay until I get back. I tucked the kids in before I left, didn't tell them I was leaving. If they know Alice is there, they'll keep getting up.

It's different here at night. Much quieter, of course, but it's more than that. The air feels charged, mysterious. There's a little nightlight on in Jay's room, and I'm sitting here in the chair watching him by its soft glow. I haven't said anything yet. I was thinking I'd tell him about Alice and Ed, but that doesn't seem like the thing to talk about. So I'm just watching.

The door pushes open and Wanda comes in with a flashlight. When she sees me sitting in the chair, she turns it off, walks over to me, and whispers, 'Hello.'

'Hi.'

'Are you staying?'

'You mean . . . all night?'

'Yes.'

'No.'

'Oh. Well, you can.'

Our whispering seems strange. Isn't he sleeping all the time? Why don't we always whisper? On the other hand, it seems respectful to me that we would treat nighttime as nighttime.

'Are you the only one here?' I ask.

'No, there are a couple of aides working with me. But I'm the only nurse. It's going to be wild tonight. Always is, when there's a full moon.'

'Is that really true? That's what Gloria said.'

'Sure. Everything happens on full-moon nights. The ones who are a little crazy go really berserk. Mrs Eliot has been carrying on since the sun set.'

'Well,' I say. 'I'll take care of Jay. You don't have

to worry about him. I'll let you know when I leave. But maybe I will stay all night.'

'Lie down with him if you want to,' Wanda says.

That has never occurred to me. The whole time he's been like this, it hasn't occurred to me to lie beside him. 'Yes, all right,' I say. 'Maybe I will.'

'Just let me do something first,' Wanda says. She moves to the side of Jay's bed, pulls down the sheet. He is on his side, and she removes the pillow supporting him, holds him over with one hand while with the other she reaches for the bottle of lotion on his bedside stand. She's proud of the way Jay's skin has held up, no bedsores yet. She squirts some lotion into one hand, closes the bottle again and puts it back on the bedside stand. Nurses are good at this kind of thing, using one hand for things that normally require two. And if you get one like Wanda, you can see the caring along with the skill. She rubs Jay's back with strong, circular strokes, and I watch, spellbound. There is a mesmerizing quality to watching someone do almost anything with care: tailors in their dry-cleaner windows, hunched over sewing machines. Bakers making art out of frosting. Children with a new pack of crayons and fierce intent. We are meant to use what we have, whatever it is. We are meant to be less mindful of our insides, more outwardly directed. That's what I think, as I watch Wanda rub Jay down, as the minty smell of the lotion makes its way over to me. There is incredible value in being in service to others. I think if most of the people in therapy offices were dragged out to put their finger in a dike, take up their place in a working line, they would be relieved of terrible burdens. I always picture someone smartly dressed, their expensive briefcase at their feet, their finger in the hole, saying, 'Oh. Well, this is better! I only needed to be essential.'

Wanda positions Jay on his back, uses a kind of swab to clean around his feeding tube, then covers it with a four-by-four and white tape. She uses another kind of swab to clean out his mouth. Then she looks over at me for a long minute. 'I think I'm going to take his catheter out,' she says. 'He's due for a change anyway.'

I sit up straighter, my mouth dry. 'All right.'

'I'll be right back. I need a syringe.'

I sit motionless until she returns, then watch as she uses the syringe to deflate the little bulb of saline that holds the catheter in Jay's bladder. She positions herself so that I don't have to watch the tube come out. It bothers me to see that, even though all the nurses have told me it's not painful in any way. 'Just one more minute,' Wanda says. She wraps the whole apparatus up in a towel, carries it out into the hall, then returns, turns on the tap in the little sink in Jay's room. She starts to wet a washcloth, then looks over at me. '. . . unless you want to do this.'

'Do what?' I say. 'What are you doing?'

'Just washing him a little. Where the tube came out.'

'Yes, all right,' I say. 'I can do it.'

'Call me if you need me. Otherwise, I won't come in. No one will.'

I want to say, I know what you've got in mind, Wanda. Just forget it. Really. I mean, what do you think? What can you be thinking? But she is gone, and the washcloth hangs on the side of the sink. I wet it with warm water, go over to Jay, and, looking out the window, wash him off quickly. Then, since there is no towel, I dry him with the sheet. 'There,' I whisper. 'I'll bet that feels better, huh?'

His hair is sticking up a little in the back. He looks like Alfalfa. I turn on the bedside lamp, find his comb in his drawer. His hair is getting longer. He needs a trim. He has beautiful blond hair, streaked like a model. They keep it clean here, at least. At the hospital, he hardly ever got his hair washed. I lean down, kiss the top of his head. He smells like himself, which seems astonishing to me. I kiss his nose, his ear. Then I straighten, run my finger down the side of his cheek. 'Jay?' I say. 'If you'll just wake up and start eating, we can get rid of the other tube. And you can come home.' I sit beside him. 'Jay, if you could just . . . Can't you let me know? Can't you tell me?'

I have to be careful. I have to be wordless. The outstretched hands drop everything, not seeing it. Never seeing it. Though they have been asking since the pyramids. Since the learning of fire. Since the first blink of the first eye.

'Jay?'

Lainey.

I'm so tired I'm dizzy. I think about getting in bed with him, but I can't. It's just too strange. I go back to the chair, sit quietly, look again at my watch even though I just looked at it. I take my shoes off, slide my feet under me, watch Jay, listen to his breathing. Then I get up and go into his drawer again, find his aftershave. I love his aftershave. He orders it from somewhere in Bermuda. It's a light, seductive scent, the kind you want to lean in and smell deeper, which is the idea, I suppose. I put a little on my fingers, rub it on his face. He lies there, motionless. It's such an odd sensation, doing things for people in a coma that they can't do for themselves. Even though you're helping them, you feel a little as though you're being cruel to them. It's that you could do anything, and they couldn't protest. They are in a state of constant vulnerability.

I lean down, sniff. Not enough aftershave. Jay used to pour aftershave in his hand, then slap it on, as men do. They have a robust approach to scenting themselves. It's so no one will think they're wimps, I guess. Well, they're right, you would think differently about a man who applied scent to his pulse points with his index finger. I pour a small puddle of aftershave in the palm of my hand, try to pat it on Jay's face, but it mostly falls onto his neck, pools in the tender indentation below his Adam's apple. 'Sorry,' I say. 'I'm sorry.' I use his sheet to blot at it. 'I guess you have to do it faster. I'm sorry.' He does smell good now, though.

I look down at his still face, then at his arms, at his beautiful hands. I liked holding hands with him at the movies. It seemed as sexual as anything else we ever did. More so, in fact. His thumb would move, just slightly, to caress one of my fingers. He'd squeeze, just a little, then let go, caress my finger again. Sometimes he'd open my hand to gently rake his fingers across my palm and a kind of shock would run up my arm and into my shoulder. He knew about the power of being gentle.

I lower the bed rail, sit down beside him, remove, with some effort, his pajama top, then his pajama bottoms. I kiss his mouth. His lips smell like lemon-glycerin swabs. I don't like that smell. I blot at his mouth with the edge of the pillowcase. Then I kiss him again. And then I unbutton my blouse and take it off. I stand to take off my jeans and then, quickly, everything else, go over to the chair and lay my things there. I have my arms wrapped around myself as I make my way back to Jay's bedside; I have never felt quite so naked. What if someone comes in? Well, he is my husband. But this is a nursing home. I get in bed with Jay, then get out again. I'll move the chair over, block the door with it. I see my breasts swinging in the moonlight as I push the chair across the floor. I think this image might be funny, later, but now it feels grotesque. Still, the chair will give me some peace of mind. At least this way, I'll have some warning. 'One minute,' I'll say.

After the chair is in place, I stretch out beside Jay, pull the sheet over both of us. I lay my head on his shoulder, rest my arm gently across his stomach. 'Hey, Jay,' I say. 'Want to hear something?' I clear my throat. And then I sing softly, 'Today I got up, and the first thing I did . . .' I swallow, continue singing, 'The first thing I did is miss you. That's all I do. I just miss you.' I feel the tears start, for the aching familiarity of all this, the feel of his flesh next to mine. I let my hand wander everywhere on him. 'Jay,' I say into his ear. 'Remember? It's me, Lainey.' Down the hall, I hear Mrs Eliot screaming, 'Vixens! Get out of my house! I'll call the police!' I lay my hand against the middle of Jay's chest, feel the movement of his soft breathing. That is the only movement there is. I imagine Jay's arm waking up suddenly to pull me closer, the slight pressure I'd feel, the stunning relief. What would I say? I think. What would he? What words would be important enough to use? I wait, but no movement comes. I reach for the angle of his jaw, rest my fingers behind it to feel the pulse in his neck. 'You smell good, Jay,' I tell him. I move my leg up to lie across his. I want a solid line of connection between our two bodies, no breaks. I breathe in deeply, sigh, close my eyes and hold as still as he does. I hold so still that I begin to feel disoriented. I feel as though I suddenly hear everything, including the absence of sound. And then I feel dizzy, as though I am falling backward into a soft space where only thought exists.

231

Come.

I startle, open my eyes, reorient myself. Then I close them again, settle my head into Jay's shoulder, begin to time my breathing to his. There. We can have that.

Inside my head, I start to see things, the warm-up show I have every night before I fall asleep, the parade of images that begins with things I can understand, then cannot. It is a very mysterious place we go to, when we go to sleep. I breathe in, breathe out. I say, 'I love you, Jay.' The sound of my words hangs in the room, seems to hover above us like a cloud with arms that reach down. We breathe in, breathe out. *We* do. I can't tell whose breath sounds are whose, and I am aware, as I feel myself falling asleep, of my gratitude at having this small communion, at being once again in this place of peace.

Six-thirty, my watch says. And at the same time I look at it, I realize where I am. At some point during the night, I turned away from Jay; I can feel him behind me. I turn quickly toward him now, look to see if the power of my presence has done anything. Apparently not. He lies still, eyes closed, presents me with the same weary blankness I've been studying for so long now.

I've slept wrong: my neck hurts, my back. I sit up, stretch, which only makes things hurt more. Then I get out of bed to collect my clothes. It's warm in the room, stale-seeming. After I'm dressed, I open the drapes, then the window. As though it has been waiting outside, a breeze rushes in. I cover Jay, kiss his temple. 'I'll be back this afternoon,' I tell him.

Why isn't this mouth opening? What is that smell, this silken air? Down and down. Lost.

Out in the hall, I see Wanda pushing the

medication cart toward me. She nods at me, smiles.

'You have to give people pills this early?' I ask.

'Sure. Seven o'clocks. Mostly antibiotics. You have to start now to get done by seven-thirty.'

'I'll bet people are really happy about that.'

'Yeah, especially Mrs Eliot.' Wanda holds up a bandaged finger. 'She bit me.'

'Are you kidding?'

'No. She's done it before.'

'But . . . Isn't it dangerous? I mean, aren't people bites worse than dog bites?'

'I washed it out right away. I poured alcohol on it, too. Hurt like hell. It's all right now. How did you do last night? Did you sleep?'

'Yeah, I did. I need to get home, though. I didn't tell my neighbor I'd be gone so long.' I hope *she* slept, I think.

When I am almost to the door, I see Flozell wheeling slowly down the hall yawning. When he sees me, he yells, 'You here already?'

'I'm just leaving.'

'Leaving! You been here all night?'

It seems a little inappropriate to me for us to be talking so loudly at this time of day. I walk over to him, say quietly, 'Yes, I slept here.'

'No fooling. In the bed? With your husband?'

'Well.'

'That's all right, Peaches. That's a good idea. There's nothing wrong with that.'

'I know that, Flozell.'

'Did it help?'

234

'No.' I look at my watch. 'What are you doing up so early anyway?'

'Oh, this my time. This my best hour! I get up, take a big long piss – sorry, but you know that's it – and then I go watch the sun come up in the day room. I do it every morning. Be my peaceful time. After this, all hell breaks out, they be getting those old skeletons up and out, line 'em up in their wheelchairs, feed 'em their mush 'fore they take 'em to the car wash. They look bad, 'fore they washed! Their hair be sticking out from the sides of their heads, look like they seen a ghost.'

'I really have to go. Speaking of breakfast.' Speaking of ghosts. 'I've got to get the kids up.'

He wheels along beside me. 'Johnny got your husband a little something. Bought him a wind chime.'

'She did?'

'Yeah, it's in my room. She was in Chinatown, she thought he might like one. Might like the sound.'

'Well, that's . . . Please tell her thank you. I'll tell her. I'll be back this afternoon, and we'll hang it up. Thank you.'

Jay's room is full of the kindness of people he's never met. It seems a miracle to me, living in what the world has become, that there could be such overt, free caring, such loving generosity. If Jay wakes up, I'm making a turkey and having all these people over for dinner. 'This is Gloria,' I'll tell Jay. 'She brought you a geranium.' Maybe he'll know. Maybe he'll be standing there with his arm around me – God! With his working arm around me! – and he'll say, 'Yes. I remember when she brought it in. I heard her.'

'She got voodoo in her background, old Johnny,' Flozell says.

'Does she?'

'I'm not lying. She got folks in New Orleans do things to you, you never know what hit you. She put a spell on me, tell you that, look like it make me crazy 'bout her for the rest of this natural life. I'm a dead man.'

'I thought you had a lot of girlfriends, Flozell.'

'I do. But she's the *main* one. Other ones, they come and go. Johnny's the permanent variety. She have the children.'

'I see.'

I am at the door, see the red sun rising up over the horizon. 'There it is,' I say, and Flozell nods; says, for once, nothing.

Alice is sleeping, her mouth open slightly. I tiptoe past her, go into the kitchen, sit wearily at the table. Nothing works. Nothing I do works.

'You can't force miracles,' I hear Evie say. 'You just need to stay out of the way for when they want to come.' She is standing at the sink, the light from the window outlining her square-shouldered blouse, her plain blue skirt. 'I nearly lost a daughter. My middle girl, Patricia. She was the one who liked to play in the pantry, used to sit on the floor in the corner, pretending. She'd take my purse, put my scarf on her head, my heels on over her socks. Then she'd go and sit in the corner, arms out in front of her. I guess she was driving, I don't know, she wouldn't ever say what she was doing, she was awful shy.

'She got pneumonia one winter. She woke up one night and she just couldn't breathe. I never saw Walter so scared as the night we brought her down to the hospital. They were taking so long to fill out the forms when we registered. And he finally got real mad, and he stood up and hiked up his pants and said, "Evie, you stay here and do this; I'm taking this child up to see a doctor right now." And he just took her in his arms and went on up to the children's ward, didn't listen to what anyone was trying to tell him. Everyone thought she would die, she was so bad off. But she didn't. There was a day she just turned the corner. No reason for it, they said. But I thought there was a reason. I thought it was something we were given, and that it was for a reason.'

I sigh, shake my head.

'Don't you lose your faith. You have a good life, and you're not finished together. You know, I like how you two talk, how you say so many things. That's important. We had a hard time with that, my husband and I. We didn't say too much, I guess we kind of kept things to ourselves. I think the best we ever did at talking was once when we were fighting. It was the worst fight we ever had, and do you know I have no memory of what it was about? No memory at all. I just know we were so angry! He'd gone stomping outside to sit on the porch, to cool off. I was in the living room, sitting in the dark; I'd turned off the light. I didn't want any lights on. I didn't know whether to cry or yell out loud. I had my fists balled up in my lap, didn't know what to do. I thought maybe I'd call my sister Irene in Chicago, she never did marry. "Come ahead," she'd say; I knew she'd say that.

But then Walter and I began to talk, just our voices floating through the screen back and forth. Neither of us could see each other. Well, I could see a kind of dark hulk out there on the porch swing. I could see the smoke from his cigarette rising up. But you know, I think it was the cover of the dark that let us talk that night, say things we hadn't said before. We started with how angry we were, but then it changed into something so nice. Kind of romantic. And he had just come in the door, he was coming back inside, pushing his hair down in the back like he did when he was feeling a little shy. But right then one of the kids came down for a drink, little Billy, he was always so thirsty at night, and he wouldn't drink bathroom water. Thought it was different. And my husband looked at me like his mouth was full of words he was dying to say but then he put his hand on Billy's shoulder, went with him into the kitchen. I heard them talking. I heard Billy's sleepy voice asking a question and my husband answering him, I heard the tap turn on and the water fill the glass. And that seemed to me to be all we needed to say. Any more, why, I think it would have been too much.'

I stand up, stare at the coffee pot, think whether I should make some or go back to bed.

'Might as well stay up, now,' Evie says.

Exactly what I'd decided. Start the coffee, take a shower, pretend I've slept just fine, sometimes that actually works. I reach through her to the sink to fill up the pot with water and she disappears like steam on the bathroom mirror, first her edges, then all of her. This is something I've never seen. In the midst of all this spectacular unreality, something new. I get the feeling that she won't be back. I don't know whether to feel comforted or abandoned. I stand still, see the sun coming through the water in the glass pot I'm holding. Yes, she's gone. Why, I wonder.

Floating through the middle, pulled. The sights of life on either side. Me, in a corner, in the dark, hunched over on a chair too small for me. I can see Lainey standing so close, her hair lit up, her face turned slightly away. I can't open my mouth to call to her. But here: I feel a slow lifting, a peeling away of the veil. And there, I see. Oh. Oh.

At seven-thirty, Alice comes into the kitchen, her hand at her back like a bad actress playing an old woman. She looks like hell – face creased, eyes swollen. She slept about as well as I did.

'I'm sorry,' I say.

'What are you sorry about?'

'That I stayed there so long.'

'I thought you might. It's fine.' She pours herself a cup of coffee, sits down with me, takes a sip. 'Ugh.'

'It's too old. I'll make more.'

'Please! God, this is awful. This is like—'

'All right!'

I dump out the coffee, start a new pot while Alice watches in silence.

'Were you awfully uncomfortable on that sofa?' I ask.

'Let's see. Yes. But you were in a chair all night. Couldn't have been any better.'

'No, I wasn't in a chair.'

She looks up at me. 'Weren't you at the nursing home?'

'Yes. I got in bed with him.'

'Oh. Oh! Funny, I never thought of that.'

'Me neither. Wanda did.'

'See, that's why I like her.'

I sit down at the table. 'Me too.'

'So you slept with him. God! Was it weird?'

'Kind of.'

'Did anything happen?'

'No.'

Silence. Then, 'Oh, Lainey.'

'It's all right.'

'No, it isn't.'

'Well, I guess we each have our own troubles.'

'I don't know. I don't know if I have any troubles.'

I look sharply at her.

'It's not so bad, as it happens. It's not! Maybe when the truth finally gets spoken, it's only a relief. At first, I felt awful. But I wonder now how much I felt like I was *supposed* to feel awful. I'm not so sure that I wasn't as deceitful as Ed was, in my way. It's occurred to me that maybe we picked each other because neither of us really wanted each other. Does that make any sense?'

'Oh, sure. Very clear. Very sensible.'

'I mean it, Lainey. This big a shake-up, it makes you take stock of everything, see it all in a different light. I think what I really wanted from our relationship was Timothy. And he's here. I think that's all Ed wanted too, and we spent years trying to talk ourselves into something else. At terrible cost. At terrible cost! This is better. I'll stay here; he'll go live with Mr Beautiful, and I know everybody will be all right. There are things about living alone that I look forward to.'

The phone rings, and I grab it quickly. I don't want it to wake up the kids, though it's time to get them up for school pretty soon anyway. After I say hello, I hear Wanda's voice. It is saying the most incredible thing. Though I would not have thought myself capable of it, I hear myself talking. I hear myself say, 'Alice? Can you take care of the girls a little longer?'

Her mouth becomes a straight line, and she gets up to come and stand beside me. I hear the coffeemaker gurgle at the same time she says, 'Oh God, Lainey, is he . . . Did he . . . ?'

'Thank you,' I say, into the phone, and hang it up. And then, to Alice, 'He woke up.' It's just three words, which seems amazing to me.

I have never felt the steering wheel quite the same way as I feel it now, have never been so aware of its shape and abilities. I have never stopped at red lights with such care and simultaneous impatience. 'Now, drive *care*fully!' Alice had said, and watched from the steps of the porch as I pulled out of the driveway. We agreed that I would be the one to tell the kids – later, after I saw Jay. I am less than a block away, now. The road is still black; the trees are still rooted. I'm not sure that my head is not going to explode, that is the feeling. I wipe away tears from my face; that's not the way I want him to see me. It's bad enough that my hair is in a wet braid, that I have no makeup on. I'd thought I might look beautiful, when this moment came.

No one is in sight when I come in the door, and though my impulse is to run down the hall, I don't. I walk. I bite my lips and feel as though my breath is captured inside me like a big square box with sharp corners. When I get to his room, I push open the door and there he is, sitting up in bed, being examined by a doctor, a woman I've never seen before. He turns, sees me, and I stop walking. My knees are becoming unreliable; I drop my purse to get rid of the weight so that I can make my way to his side.

'We can talk later,' the doctor says, putting her ophthalmoscope into her pocket. 'Why don't you just take a little time, now?'

'Yes,' Jay says, and the sound of his voice makes my hand go up to my mouth. 'Lainey?' he says then, and though I didn't want him to see me crying, that is all I can do, I go over and hold him against me, and I weep so loudly I think I might crack the walls. I don't know the words for this. I only know the feeling. It is over me like a blanket, in me like blood.

Epilogue

It is fall, and I'm working a lot of hours at
Beverage World. Business has picked up; Frank
may have to hire another person. Dolly has
insisted that this time she does all the interview-
ing, and he has agreed. Although we usually eat at
our desks, I had lunch out with Dolly last week,
and she told me about her new boyfriend. 'He's
nothing like Frank,' she said, 'but he's a real nice
man. We have a good time together.' She was
looking out the window when she told me that,
and I saw reflected in her bifocals a couple
walking down the street, arms around each other.
'Well,' she said, looking back at me. 'You know, at
some point, you just have to move on.' I smiled,
nodded. I felt so badly for her, sitting there in her
powder-blue cardigan and smelling only slightly
of a safe perfume. But she does not seem unhappy;
she continues to enjoy the little relationship she
has with Frank, and I have come to see that in the

way they are able, they love each other. He notices anything new she comes in with, from a piece of jewelry to shoes to a slightly runny nose; she continues to carry his coffee in to him and I am careful to never put phone calls through at that time. There was a Friday when she was in there a good twenty minutes, and she came out with a color in her face that I thought made her beautiful.

Jay is back to work almost full-time. He lost quite a bit of function in one arm and he goes for therapy at the hospital every afternoon. They say in a week or two he'll be all done, good as new.

It was a funny thing when he came home. Amy was afraid of him for a long time, weeks. I think she saw him as risen from the dead. Well, so did I, I guess. I was afraid he'd fall back into a coma; for a long time, I'd wake up several times a night and make him wake up too. Finally we were both exhausted, and Jay asked me, in the gentlest of ways, to cut it out. He doesn't recall anything specifically from when he was in a coma: for him, it was a long, strange nap. 'Cinnamon?' I'll say. 'Do you remember smelling cinnamon?', and he'll say, '. . . No. Was there cinnamon there?' He does occasionally have a shiver of something, though, a gloved tap. He says it's a feeling of nearly remembering something, then not. Losing it. He describes it as the way that none of us can remember being born, and yet we do seem to re-member anyway, in that nearly all of us have a vague longing to go back somewhere. Jay says what else can it be but the womb, where all our

248

needs were met before we knew we had them? I suppose that might be true, although my fantasy as a child was that I was from a superior planet whose most important members would soon come to reclaim me, hopefully when I was in Mrs Menafee's geometry class where, due to certain mathematical failings, I functioned as inadvertent class clown. I waited every day for people dressed in silver to walk into the classroom and astonish her – and save me. I intended to ask what took them so long.

I told Jay all that I remembered about him being in the hospital, then in the nursing home. I had that turkey dinner for all the people who took care of him at the nursing home, too. I had to have it at the home, in the rec room, because otherwise a lot of people would have been working and wouldn't have been able to come to our house. Gloria and Wanda and Pat, all Jay's nurses came up and told him they were the ones who did this and that, and Jay listened in a kind of polite wonder. Flozell smacked him on the back and sat beside him the whole time; it was like they were war buddies. Jay goes to visit Flozell at least once a week or so now, and Amy goes along most of the time.

It took me a while to tell Jay about seeing Evie. It was a Sunday night; we'd had Chinese food just like we always used to. The kids were in bed, and the little white boxes were all over the family room, sauces thickening at the bottoms. Jay started to clean up and I told him no, just to wait a minute, I wanted to sit there with him for a while and think about how happy I was that we were doing this again. He put his arm around me and we had our stocking feet up on the coffee table and I said, 'You know, when you were gone, I had regular hallucinations. I saw a ghost, a ghost woman.' He pulled away, looked down into my face, concerned. 'No,' I said, 'it wasn't a bad thing. She actually helped. She talked to me, made me feel better.' He wanted to know what she said, and I told him mostly just things that happened in this house, in this neighborhood. 'Like what?' he'd said, and I told him about how there was a war bride from Japan a few doors down who'd renamed herself Shirley and who kept trying to whip cream with chopsticks, so the women in the neighborhood chipped in and got her a mixer. I told him about how Walter once came downstairs after he'd put the kids to bed, changed into his best suit, slicked his hair back. Evie was in the kitchen, finishing the dishes. He'd called her into the living room, turned on the radio, low, then bowed and asked her to dance. She'd felt a little embarrassed, but then she'd taken off her apron and her glasses, slid out of her shoes, turned off most of the lights, and stepped into Walter's arms for Harry James and 'I'll Get By.' 'Huh,' Jay had said. 'That's nice.' He'd looked at me for a long time after that, checking to see if I was all right, I guess.

It was about a month after he was home that we finally had a fight, Jay and I. I have to say it was what let me know he was really back, that I could relax. I slammed the door and went over to Alice's house and told her Jay was an asshole. She poured us glasses of wine and toasted me. She's doing so well, Alice. I've met Ed's lover, Sloan, and I like him. I asked Alice if Sloan was his real name or if it used to be Elmer and she said who knew. I know it's an awful cliché, but Ed seems to have blossomed, really, to have opened up into himself, and he's so much easier to be with. I'm not sure what the kids really think; I know they talk about it, but not around me. I tried to eavesdrop once, and they caught me, which is pretty embarrassing.

Alice is dating a gorgeous-looking Chinese man who teaches astrophysics over at the university. Their favorite thing to do is go roller-skating at the big wooden rinks a few blocks away. I don't know. You tell me. He appreciates her; it's a pleasure to see the way he watches her talking, the careful way he takes her hand. And she tells me he is the most fantastic lover. She won't give me too many details, which I think might be the sign of something really special. Still, I keep after her. I'm dying to know.

Sometimes when I'm alone in the house I kind of ask for Evie to come back, but she never does. I wish she would. I want to tell her something. I want to tell her about the day Jay came home, what it was like when he opened the door to his house and walked back in. How he stood for a long moment in the hall, and didn't say anything. There were, of course, no words. There was just the slow lifting of his hand to the familiar banister at the foot of the stairs, the glint of the wedding ring that has never left his finger since the day I put it there. I want to say that I understood something at that moment, which was this: the gift is not that I got to bring Jay back. The gift is that I know what I brought him back to; and so does he. I suppose Evie knew that, though. I think that was all she was ever really saying.

And so I am out here on the wooden stoop in my sweater worn thin at the elbows, and it is early morning, and I am looking out at my own back-yard and at the trees beyond that and at the sky beyond that and I am thinking this:

I am living on a planet where the silk dresses of Renaissance women rustled, where people died in plagues, where Mozart sat to play, where sap runs in the spring, where children are caught in crossfire, where gold glints from rock, where religion shines its light only to lose its way, where people stop to reach a hand to help each other to cross, where much is known about the life of the ant, where the gift of getting my husband back was as accidental as my almost losing him, where the star called sun shows itself differently at every hour, where people get so bruised and confused they kill each other, where baobabs grow into impossible shapes with trunks that tell stories to hands, where rivers wind wide and green with terrible hidden currents, where you rise in the morning and feel your own arms with your own hands, checking yourself, where lovers' hearts swell with the certain knowledge that only they are the ones, where viruses are seen under the insistent eye of the microscope and the birth of stars is witnessed through the lens of the tele-scope, where caterpillars crawl and skyscrapers are erected because of the blue line on the blue-print – I am living here on this planet, it is my time to have my legs walk the earth, and I am turning around to tell Jay once again, 'Yes, here.' I am saying that all of this, all of this, all of these things are the telling songs of the wider life, and I am listening with gratitude, and I am listening for as long as I can, and I am listening with all of my might.

THE END

Talk Before Sleep
Elizabeth Berg

'A RICH COMING-OF-AGE NOVEL . . . A LUMINOUS
WORK'
New York Times Book Review

*'Until that moment, I hadn't realized how much I'd been
needing to meet someone I might be able to say everything
to . . .'*

Ann and Ruth have always talked as only great friends can –
honestly, and about everything: husbands and marriages, sex
lives and children, their work, their hopes, their
disappointments, and their dreams. For Ann, cautious and
conventional, her closeness to the outspoken and eccentric
Ruth brings about discovery, a chance to say whatever she
wants, and, most important, under the insistent tutelage of
Ruth, to become herself. Over the years, the women have
shared recipes, child care, delicate and dangerous secrets and
each rests secure in the knowledge that they will be friends
forever. But then, everything changes; faced with a crisis that
redefines the meaning of friendship, they begin to share
something more profound than either of them might have
predicted.

Written with an unerring ear for how women talk, laugh, and
cry together, and with a gift for capturing the magical
uniqueness of personality, *Talk Before Sleep* is sure to find a
place in readers' hearts.

'A SEARING STORY OF FRIENDSHIP AND DEATH
AMONG FORTY-SOMETHING FEMALES . . . A TRIUMPH
OF CREATIVITY'
Time Out

0 553 40956 5

A BANTAM PAPERBACK

The Book Of Ruth
Jane Hamilton

'HAMILTON'S STORY BUILDS TO A SHOCKING
CRESCENDO. HER SMALL-TOWN CHARACTERS ARE AS
APPEALINGLY OFFBEAT AND BRUSHED WITH GRACE
AS ANY FOUND IN ALICE HOFFMAN'S OR ANNE
TYLER'S NOVELS'
Glamour

Pegged as the loser in a small-town family, Ruth grows up,
unlovely and unloved – and in the shadow of her brilliant
brother. With no ticket out of Honey Creek, she cleaves to her
tough and bitter mother, May, and tries to keep the peace
between her and Ruby, the sweet but slightly deranged man
she marries and supports.

But when the precarious household erupts in violence, it is
Ruth who is left to piece their story together – and she gets at
the truth in a manner at once ferocious, hilarious, and
heartbreaking.

'AN AMERICAN BEAUTY THIS BOOK . . . SENSATIONAL
FIRST NOVEL'
Vogue

'A NEW AND ORIGINAL VOICE IN FICTION'
Boston Sunday Globe

Previously published in Great Britain as *The Frogs are Still
Singing*

0 552 99685 8

BLACK SWAN

A SELECTED LIST OF FINE WRITING
AVAILABLE FROM BLACK SWAN AND BANTAM BOOKS

THE PRICES SHOWN BELOW WERE CORRECT AT THE TIME OF GOING TO PRESS. HOWEVER TRANSWORLD PUBLISHERS RESERVE THE RIGHT TO SHOW NEW RETAIL PRICES ON COVERS WHICH MAY DIFFER FROM THOSE PREVIOUSLY ADVERTISED IN THE TEXT OR ELSEWHERE.

99313	1	OF LOVE AND SHADOWS	Isabel Allende	£6.99
99564	9	JUST FOR THE SUMMER	Judy Astley	£5.99
99618	1	BEHIND THE SCENES AT THE MUSEUM	Kate Atkinson	£6.99
40956	5	TALK BEFORE SLEEP	Elizabeth Berg	£5.99
99648	3	TOUCH AND GO	Elizabeth Berridge	£5.99
99593	2	A RIVAL CREATION	Marika Cobbold	£5.99
99692	0	THE PRINCE OF TIDES	Pat Conroy	£6.99
99587	8	LIKE WATER FOR CHOCOLATE	Laura Esquivel	£6.99
99622	X	THE GOLDEN YEAR	Elizabeth Falconer	£5.99
99488	X	SUGAR CAGE	Connie May Fowler	£5.99
99599	1	SEPARATION	Dan Franck	£5.99
99610	6	THE SINGING HOUSE	Janette Griffiths	£5.99
99685	8	THE BOOK OF RUTH	Jane Hamilton	£6.99
99391	3	MARY REILLY	Valerie Martin	£4.99
99503	7	WAITING TO EXHALE	Terry McMillan	£5.99
99506	1	BETWEEN FRIENDS	Kathleen Rowntree	£5.99
99672	6	A WING AND A PRAYER	Mary Selby	£6.99
99607	6	THE DARKENING LEAF	Caroline Stickland	£5.99
99650	5	A FRIEND OF THE FAMILY	Titia Sutherland	£5.99
99130	9	NOAH'S ARK	Barbara Trapido	£6.99
99549	5	A SPANISH LOVER	Joanna Trollope	£6.99
99636	X	KNOWLEDGE OF ANGELS	Jill Paton Walsh	£5.99
99673	4	DINA'S BOOK	Herbjørg Wassmo	£6.99
99592	4	AN IMAGINATIVE EXPERIENCE	Mary Wesley	£5.99
99639	4	THE TENNIS PARTY	Madeleine Wickham	£5.99
99591	6	A MISLAID MAGIC	Joyce Windsor	£4.99

All Transworld titles are available by post from:
Book Service By Post, PO Box 29, Douglas, Isle of Man IM99 1BQ
Credit cards accepted. Please telephone 01624 675137, fax 01624 670923 or Internet http://www.bookpost.co.uk for details.
Please allow £0.75 per book for post and packing UK.
Overseas customers allow £1 per book for post and packing.